William Carleton

Redmond Count O'Hanlon, the Irish Rapparee

An Historical Tale

William Carleton

Redmond Count O'Hanlon, the Irish Rapparee
An Historical Tale

ISBN/EAN: 9783744725552

Printed in Europe, USA, Canada, Australia, Japan

Cover: Foto ©Andreas Hilbeck / pixelio.de

More available books at **www.hansebooks.com**

REDMOND

COUNT O'HANLON,

The Irish Rapparee.

An Historical Tale.

BY

WILLIAM CARLETON,

Author of "Valentine McClutchy," "Tales and Stories of the Irish Peasantry,"
"The Tithe Proctor," "Art Maguire," "Willy Reilly," "Fardo-
rougha, the Miser," "The Black Prophet," "The Black
Baronet," "Jane Sinclair," "The Emi-
grants of Ahadarra," "The
Evil Eye," &c.

NEW YORK:
P. J. KENEDY,
EXCELSIOR PUBLISHING HOUSE,
5 BARCLAY STREET.
1896.

REDMOND COUNT O'HANLON,

THE IRISH RAPPAREE.

CHAPTER I.

A HAPPY FIRESIDE, WITH A MARRIAGE IN THE DISTANCE.

In the year of grace sixteen hundred and ninety-six, there lived not far from the northern base of Slievegullion mountain a very wealthy farmer named Callan, who was father to one daughter named Rose, his eldest child, and three sons, none of whom had grown beyond boyhood. This man held a farm of two hundred and sixty acres of excellent land, at a very light rent, and lived in rude abundance and comfort. We must admit, however, that if it were not for a certain compact into which he had entered with a man whose reputation at that time had become known throughout Europe, it would be impossible for us to say that he could have lived under anything like a sense of security so far as his property, at least, was concerned. Of this, however, more hereafter. This farmer, by name Brian Callan, was laborious, simple-hearted, and honest; an affectionate husband, a fond father, and an obliging neighbor. His wife was a Duffy, and on the surface of this earth there breathed not a woman gifted with more of those virtues which adorn and shed their pure and holy lustre upon domestic life. Honesty, charity, simplicity, piety, and affection, all mingled and supported each other in her character, and made her name a household world of praise for many a mile around her happy dwelling. We will not fatigue our readers with an elaborate description of their daughter Rose. There are plenty of such descriptions in the novels, although you could not probably find one of them suitable to her. She was about the middle size, had rich dark auburn hair, was exquisitely shaped, had a sweet oval face, a beautiful mouth, and soft, dark, mellow eyes; and there, as to figure and beauty, is all we will or can say concerning her person. In a moral point of view, there was about her a charm of artlessness that was fascinating, to which, however, was added a fund of good sense and spirit that excited respect from all who knew her—a proof, besides, that she possessed no ordinary degree of firm principle and stability of character. She was at this period of our story only nineteen.

Not far from her father's house lived another family named M'Mahon, belonging to the great stock of the M'Mahons of Monaghan. They also were wealthy; for, like the family of the Callans, of whom we write, they had kept themselves aloof from the disturbances of the preceding times, and each consequently bore a character of inoffensive peacefulness and industry. Art M'Mahon had three sons, two of whom were already married and comfortably settled in their own houses. His youngest son, Con, who still lived with him, was unmarried; and, as it was then customary among his class, he was the individual into whose hands his father's farm should descend at his death. Con M'Mahon then was, at the period when our narrative commences, the betrothed, and, need we say, the accepted lover of Rose Callan, generally known, in consequence of her extraordinary beauty, as the "Fair Rose of Lisbuy"—Lisbuy signifying the Yellow Fort, so called from the fact of its being overgrown with broom; and from this Fort, or Forth, as it is termed by the people, the whole townland had its name.

It has been observed for centuries, and is, we believe, true to the present day, that of all the clans or septs of the Irish people, the M'Mahons, both men and women, stand unrivaled for personal beauty. Nobody can say that they ever saw a M'Mahon ill-shaped or ugly—at least we ourselves never did, although we have seen as many of them as most people living. Con M'Mahon was no exception to this general rule ; for, indeed, it would be a difficult thing to see a finer-looking or handsomer young fellow in his native barony.

Those two families were at this time very happy. The arrangement for the marriage of the "Fair Rose of Lisbuy" and young Con M'Mahon had been completed, and nothing now remained but the ordinary preparations for that happy event

The state of Ireland at this time, though not marked by the dreadful convulsions which had wasted and distracted it not long before, was still far from being peaceful or settled. Property was very unsafe ; for although the turbulent outrages that had spread about desolation upon a more fearful scale, had somewhat diminished, still there were too many of those violent and lawless spirits abroad to allow the peaceable and quiet, especially if they possessed wealth or property, to sleep in their beds with anything like a sense of security.

Not very far from Lisbuy lived a family named Johnston, who were then claiming some property which had been forfeited by the O'Hanlons, of Tandragee, a Catholic family, who had fought under James's banner at the battle of the Boyne, where several of them fell in that unsuccessful struggle. This family was a branch of the celebrated Johnstons of the Fews— Protestants of great energy and spirit, and who had very much distinguished themselves in suppressing the outrages which, even then, disturbed that part of the country. A young man belonging to the branch we have alluded to, and

who held a commission in the king's army, was at that time
residing with a detachment of his regiment, which was then
lying in the barracks of Armagh. This young soldier, with
the exception of an occasional chase after the Rapparees, had
never been engaged in actual service. He was, however, of
loose and licentious principles, and spent a good deal of his
time in profligacy or debauchery of the worst description.
Whilst lying in Armagh with his party, he was in the habit
of riding frequently to his father's house, and at the same time
reconnoitering the country for his victims. Every army, in
every age and country, has produced men of this detestable
character; and, indeed, in any army, or in any country, it
would be difficult to find a more unscrupulous villain than
young William Lucas. God had endowed him with certain
high gifts, which he prostituted to the basest and most profligate purposes. Being handsome, accomplished, and wealthy,
though said to be deficient in courage, he concentrated all
these advantages to that which we have stated to be the great
and immoral object of his life—reckless sensuality.

Upon one of his usual excursions to his father's house, it so
happened that he caught a glance of Rose Callan, whom he
immediately marked down as his victim. His visits home now
became very frequent; but not satisfied with this, he occasionally procured leave of absence for a week or fortnight
under various pretenses. His usual amusement was shooting,
by which he was enabled to traverse the country, and enter
the farmers' or cotters' houses, for the purpose, as the unsuspecting people thought, of asking a drink, or obtaining some
other refreshment. Among others, he soon made a point to
pay a visit of this kind to the family of Brian Callan. It is
not our intention to offend the taste of our readers by attempting to detail the arts and ingenious devices with which
he attempted to destroy the character of the pure Rose of

Lisbuy. It is sufficient to say that they were al exercised in
vain. The girl was virtuous, and what was still more against
him, imbued with a deep sense of piety and religicn. She saw
his object, and in spite of his easy and fascinating manners,
she not only despised, but abhorred and detested him. On the
last visit which, in his character of a sportsman, he ever paid
at her father's house, after having received a drink of milk, he
significantly handed her five pounds, as a reward, he said, for
ner hospitality. This she refused, adding:

"The poorest beggar, sir, that enters under our roof, would
receive the same kindness. Take back your money!"

"Not at all," said he ; "I could not think of it. Nothing
would give me more pleasure than making such presents to so
beautiful a girl as you are."

"I will receive no presents from you, sir," she replied, indignantly ; "and now, that I am alone in my father's house, it is
dishonorable in you to offer them."

He then proceeded to approach her. "Keep your distance,
sir," said she ; "don't approach me!"

He still continued, however, to draw near, when she flew to
a little cupboard that hung against the wall, and seizing an
Irish skean, she took God to witness, that if he laid a hand
upon her she would plunge it in his heart. As she uttered the
words, he saw there was that about her which could not for a
moment be misunderstood. Her fine person became strung, as
it vere, into intense vigor—her dark eyes gleamed with resolution, and the natural crimson of her cheek deepened with indignation. Lucas paused, and felt that he never admired her
so much.

"Why, my dear girl," said he, "this is a mere waste of
anger ; but indeed you look so beautiful in your indignation,
that it is almost a pity you should ever look otherwise. It is
not every day that a gentleman of my wealth and rank hap

pens to fall in love with a girl in your station of life ; yet so it is."

"Begone, sir," she replied : "begone, and take your money with you, and let this be your last visit to my father's house."

"Well, well," said he, "I will take up the money, but you will change your mind, I hope. Good bye, my beautiful girl; think of me as one who is anxious to be your friend, if you would allow him, and who would place you in a far differ ent——"

He had gone outside the door, where he stood while utter-ing the words; ere he could proceed further, however, in the vile proposal he was about to insinuate, she slapped the door indignantly in his face, and having secured it inside, she sat down and gave way to a burst of bitter tears.

"What a beautiful creature she is !" he exclaimed to him-self; "I have seen nothing like her so for——and the truth is, I must have her by hook or by crook."

This was the first occasion on which he had found Rose Callan alone in her father's house, and the reader is now cognizant of the success with which he attempted to corrupt her principles.

It was one night in the month of November, about six weeks after this event, in the year above mentioned, that Brian Callan was sitting at his comfortable hearth chatting happily with his children, his laboring servants, and a few of the neighbooring peasantry, who had come, as the phrase is, to make their *keailye* with him for an hour or two. Rose was at her distaff, inside the jamb, spinning flax, an occupation which at that time was not common even in Ireland ; her mother was grinding oats in a quern, or hand-mill, which was placed on a quilt spread over the kitchen floor, to prevent the meal from being wasted. Rose's dark auburn hair was bound by a ribbon that went round her head, but did not prevent it from falling in rich natural ringlets about her snowy white shoulders. The chimney was well lined with fat smoke-dried bacon and hung beef, and the whole house had an air of great warmth, comfort, and cleanliness. A blazing fire of turf was down, which threw its rich and mellow light throughout the whole kitchen. Rose, however, did not seem to take a very particular interest in their conversation, but seemed somewhat abstracted, if not anxious, for it might be observed that she paused as if to listen from time to time, and if a noise happened to be heard, especially near the door, she would start, and her eyes would brighten for a moment. On finding that there was nothing in it, however, she would resume her spinning, and seem somewhat cast down or disappointed.

"Come," said her father to his eldest son, a fine manly boy of thirteen, "come Owen, tell us a story."—for Owen, like many a boy of his age, was not only fond of stories, but a famous story-teller himself; in fact, quite a young Senachie.

"Come, Owen avillish, will you give us a story?" they all exclaimed; "you're the beauty of the world at it."

"Bedad, I dunna what to tell," said Owen, exceedingly proud at the time, in consequence of being selected to amuse the company; "I have none, sure."

"Oh, that indeed," exclaimed Shamus Oew (James, the son of Hugh), and you can bate Tom Gressy (the shoemaker), right and left."

"Well," said Owen, with the face of a lad who seemed demurely conscious of his own talents, "I'll try and do my best, and you all know the best can do no more."

"True enough, abouchal," said Shamus, "but at any rate make a beginnin', for you know what's well begun is half-ended."

"Well—hem," commenced Owen, clearing his throat, "There was a widow woman once, and she had three sons;

they were all very poor, but it was their own fault. The eldest was idle and undutiful, and wouldn't do anything toward
their support ; the second was as idle and undutiful as he was,
and as lazy as Harry Harvey, that could never be got to take
his shirt off to let it be washed ; the only one that ever did
anything for the family was the third and youngest of them
all, and if it hadn't been for him and his mother, they'd all
starve.   At last one mornin' the eldest says to his mother,
' Mother, bake me a bannock, and roast me a collop, till I go
and pitch (seek) my fortune.'   So his mother baked him a
bannock and roasted him a collop, that he might go and pitch
his fortune.   Well, when the bannock was baked, and he
ready to start, his mother, takin' it up, says to him, ' Now,
whether will you have the *half* of this with my blessin', or the
whole of it with my curse ?'   ' Indeed, mother,' says he, ' the
whole of it is little enough, I think, for it's a short way the
half of it would take me ; as for the curse, I'll take the whole
of the bannock and it together.'   Well, his mother gave him
the whole of the bannock sure enough ; but she stood on the
thrashil of the door, and cursed him till he got out o' sight.
Well, he went on far—farther than I can tell, till he came
to a——"

Here the latch of the kitchen door was raised, and the
next minute young Con M'Mahon made his appearance, accompanied by his father and his two brothers ; and ah, my
dear reader, maybe the eyes of the Rose of Lisbuy did not
flash and glisten, and her pure but loving heart palpitate with
ecstasy when she saw her lover and heard his voice.   Her
cheeks glowed with a blush of joy and happiness which she
could not repress, and the distaff became unmanageable in her
hands.

"God save all here !"—welcome and social words- -and
"God save you kindly !" soon passed between them.   In a

moment the company about the fire rose up in order that new
arrangements for places and accommodation might be made
The semicircle about the hearth was extended ; other seats
were drawn in ; they once more sat down ; each, of course,
comfortable ; but there was one place unanimously allowed
and reserved for the lover—and that was his usual one—on
the hob immediately behind Rose's chair. There was nothing
in this to offend Rose's delicacy. Every thing with respect
to their forthcoming marriage was known throughout the
parish, and his father and brothers accompanied him for the
purpose of settling the day for their wedding. After some
chat between the seniors present, and a low, tender dialogue
between Con and Rose, old M'Mahon at last left his seat, and
going behind the jamb returned with a jar of spirits, because,
be it known to our readers, that no negotiations of this kind
ever takes place without whisky, which, by the way, is uni-
formly provided by the bridegroom and his relatives. On this
occasion we need not say that it added very much to the
harmony and hilarity of those who were assembled, especially
upon an occasion in itself naturally festive. The conversation
was enlivened by mirth and laughter, and every one, especially
the youngsters, looked forward to the day of the wedding
with a sense of exuberant delight, which they could not restrain. At length the whisky began to circulate, and the
conversation, after bearing on many different topics, began to
to turn toward the occasion on which they were assembled :
this was simply to appoint the day on which the young couple
should be married and made happy. Some one suggested,
from a motive of comic malice, that the marriage should take
place on a Sunday ; but this was received with a clamor of
indignation that soon put an end to such a disagreeable and
unnational project. Every one krew, they said, that they
would have Sunday, whether they were married or not, and

that such an arrangement would deprive them of the benefit
of a holiday during the week ; besides, did not all the world
know that Sunday marriages were never lucky. No, no, they
would not stand *that :* and the arrangement took place accordingly.   There is, indeed, such a prejudice against marriages on the Sabbath, and some unfounded superstition exists
against them, and on this account very few marriages ever do
take place upon that day   And indeed we may remark here,
that the prejudice we speak of prevails as much in high life as
it does among the humbler classes.   Be this as it may, the
healths of the young pair were drank with all the warmth and
enthusiasm peculiar to our national character.   Other healths
also went round ; hands were grasped in cordiality and friend-
ship, and the evening closed with a short encomium : first, on
the excellent qualities and many virtues of Rose Callan by her
affectionate and admiring father.

"She is," said he, whilst the tears stood in his eyes, "she
is—but where's the use of me sayin' what she is? Doesn't
every one know it ?   There she sits ; the girl that never gave
one of us a sore heart, nor ever wanst disturbed even our
temper.   It is not the fortune that you'll get along wid her,
Con M'Mahon, for I think nothing of that, and I'm sure you
don't either."

"No, Brian, not the value of a grain of chaff," replied her
generous young lover.

"No, I knew you didn't," continued her father ; "but you
will have a fortune and what's worth a thousand fortunes besides, and that is the blessin' of God, and a pure and lovin'
heart that will make you contented and happy, even if you
had only the black wather and the dry potatoes between you.
In the meantime, you won't be brought to that, I trust.
You're both goin' together with comfortable manes, and the
free consent of your parents and friends on both sides; and

may God grant you both—as I'm sure he will—happiness and health and comfort during your lives!"

Old M'Mahon rose and grasped his hand, whilst he said—

"Every word, Brian, that has come from your lips is true, and we all know it to be so—and indeed he should be able to make a far look-out that could find a husband worthy of her. If any one is, I think my son Con comes near it—but, indeed, even he isn't."

"What's that you say?" replied her father, rising up sud-denly, "am I to understand you as layin' down to us, that your son Con there isn't worthy of her!"

"Troth he's not," rejoined his father, and I don't know the boy that is."

"*Honoman dioual*, man, don't attempt to say such a thing at my fireside. He is her fill of a husband—and fit to be a husband for a better girl than ever stood in her shoes—that is, if such a girl could be had."

"Troth an' he isn't," persisted his father; "divil a boy in the barony of Orior is worthy of her. Don't look angry, Brian. I know what I'm sayin', and I know the value of *my* son, as well as you do of *your* daughter—or may be betther, for I don't think you know the full value of your daughter yet; but if you don't, I do, and I say there's not a man in the barony of Orior worthy of her, nor in the five baronies next it—and that is more, I believe."

"Con M'Mahon, I'd contradict you, if it was the last word in my death rattle. I say, your son—sitting there before us is—and I say, if you hadn't the whisky in your head you wouldn't deny it,—and, indeed, between you and me, it's not a very fatherly thing for you to do—I know the value of my daughter well."

"I deny that, too," replied old M'Mahon; "I deny it; I say you don't know half her value"

"Why *corpan dioual*, man alive, who has a better right to know it so well—barrin', indeed, her mother—well then——"

"Ay, there is—another—that knows it better than either of you."

"Well, may be so," returned Callan, partly in a tone of irony, and partly in one of amazement at the mystery involved in M'Mahon's extraordinary line of argument; "but who might that other person be?"

"Why, then, I'll tell you; that young Cornet Lucas—but nothing, thank goodness, to the Lucases of Castleshane——"

Rose's father paused, looked about him, then at his daugh ter, whose whole neck and countenance became instantly over-spread with a deep and burning blush. His eye rested on her for a moment. Why did she blush?—here was a mystery— perhaps disgrace. His veins became tremulous with agitation, and his features the color of death. He hemmed two or three times in order to recover his breath and his voice, for both for a space had left him.

"Con M'Mahon," said he, "what is the meaning of this? My child's name is as pure as her own heart, as the snow from Heaven; beware of castin' a stain upon it, for I am, as you know, something like yourself when I'm vexed—a dangerous man; and what I might overlook in my own case, I neither could nor will in her's. Spake out; or, if you don't, I'll make you, before ever you put your head from under this roof. My child is my life, and dearer to me than it is."

"It's a terrible disclosure I have to make," replied M'Mahon, solemnly; "and as I know it may be the means of great distress to some one, I don't care if I take another glass of whisky before I spake out."

"The whisky is your own," replied Callan, "and as you have been givin' it round all the night, help yourself."

These words he uttered with a voice that was hoarse and deeply agitated.

"Well," said the other, rather coolly, filling a glass for himself at the same time, "here's all our healths, and that we may get well out of it—only, in the manetime, I wish that a person I was spaking to a few days ago was here now, that he might bear witness to the charge I'm goin' to make against—against—against who?—why, *honoman dioual*, man, against *your* daughter!"

A silence like that of death followed these words for more than a minute. The whole company seemed to be thundeistruck. Rose's mother got up and was about to approach M'Mahon, with all the indignation of a mother in her eyes, when the kitchen door opened, and a lame man, in the garb of a beggar, entered the kitchen. The moment M'Mahon saw him he started up, exclaiming—

"God is good and just; and the very man I wished to see at this moment is here. Patchy Baccach, although I'm not undher my own roof, still I'll bid you welcome. Here, man," he added, filling him a glass of spirits, "try this, and tell me first what you think of it. Afther that we want to have your opinion upon a certain subject that we wor just talkin' about, and if I don't mistake, you can throw some light upon it."

Patchy, who was called *Baccach*, in consequence of his lameness, took the glass, and was about to drink it, when Brian Callan interrupted him.

"Patchy," said he, "Con M'Mahon has bid you welcome under my roof; but before you drink that glass I wish to say that I and more bid you welcome as heartily as he did ; get a seat for Patchy there, and let him sit down."

"Many thanks to you both, gentlemen," said Patchy, taking the seat which one of the youngsters had reached him. "Many thanks to you both, and health and happiness to all of us!

What I think of it, Con M'Mahon? Oh then, death alive, what could any one think of it that tastes it, barrin' that one glass of it desarves another to the end of the chapter."

"Well, Patchy," replied M'Mahon, taking him at his word, for the hint was so well given that it was impossible to refuse him, "you must have another ; sure they'll keep one anothei company, and be neighborly where they're gone to."

Patchy having finished the second glass, and taken a view of those about him, saw at once that they appeared gloomy and evidently disturbed. He said nothing, however, but re-solved to watch the event of this agitated state of feeling, whatever it might be.

Rose's mother, however, now that this little incident had passed, approached M'Mahon, whom her husband was also approaching, but she put him aside.

"Come, now," said she, "what charge, Con M'Mahon, have you to make against our daughter?"

"Why, not much," he replied; "nothing to signify, barring to receive private visits from young Cornet Lucas undher your own roof—undher this very roof."

"Father," said her lover, getting up, "whoever told you that is a liar ; it is as false as hell—as false as the lying tongue and the black heart of the scoundrel you speak of."

Rose, seizing him by the arm, whispered to him to sit down, and to keep himself calm. "Don't be alarmed," she added, "about me. Let them finish the subject among them ; after that trust to me—to *your own* Rose."

As if overcome by the wand of an enchanter, he immediately sat down, his dark, mellow eye beaming upon her with pride, love, and confidence, which no charge or slander could shake.

"I agrev wid your son," said her father, stepping before his wife ; "the thing is a lie. He never had a private meetin' wid her undher this roof, nor anywhere else."

"I think you had betther ask herself," said the Baccach.

"Right, Patchy," said her father. "Come, Rose," he added, turning triumphantly to his daughter, "is this true? Had you ever a private meetin' wid young Cornet Lucas?"

"I had," she replied, smiling.

Her father and mother fell down suddenly on their seats and covered their faces with their hands; but her lover, on the contrary, remained calm and firm. Old M'Mahon also smiled, and, after looking significantly at the Baccach, said:

"We must have another glass on the head of this."

It was evident, however, that when he spoke in the plural number he meant no other person than himself. Having taken the glass, he proceeded:

"Now, Brian Callan, what do you say, or what can you say of the daughter you praised so highly?"

"That she's truth and honesty, M'Mahon; and that she never had, wid her own consent, a private meetin' wid him; that he used to call here when he was out shootin' to get something to refresh him, I grant, but then we were always present; and now, Con M'Mahon, lave my house, both yourself and—no; I was goin' to say your son, but I won't. No idle piece of falsehood or scandal will ever break down his love for my daughter; or if it does, then he's no longer worthy of her, and she'll have a good escape of him."

M'Mahon, after whispering a few moments with the Baccach, said:

"Well, Brian, I think we have gone far enough, maybe too far-but it is time to clear this business up. I tould you that you did'nt know half the good qualities of your daughter, and neither you do; but I have better authority ready to spake for her, and that's both an eye-witness and an ear-witness. Come, Patchy, go to work, and set all right."

To the utter astonishment of Rose, Patchy commenced and

2

gave to the whole company an accurate and detailed account
of the last visit which young Lucas had paid to her father's
house, not omitting the history of the proffered bribe, nor the
more significant episode of the skean, and the equally signifi
cant purpose for which Rose had resorted to it, winding up all
with the indignant resolution she had displayed in slapping the
door in his face, and barring it immediately afterward.

"Now !" exclaimed old M'Mahon, in triumph, "didn't I
tell you, Brian, that you knew only half the value of your
sweet girl. Come over, Rose, and kiss your father-in-law,
darlin', for it's he that will be proud of you as his daughter."

Rose complied at once, and the old man embraced her with
the most paternal tenderness, after which she returned to her
seat.

In the meantime, her father and mother felt their hearts
divided between joy and surprise.

"Why, then, Rose !" exclaimed both parents, almost at the
same moment, "why is it that you never mentioned a word
of this to us ?"

"Because," replied Rose, "I didn't wish to make either of
you uneasy. I knew very well that I taught him a lesson he
would not forget ; and knowing, as I did, from the treatment
I gave him, that he would never pay another visit to this
house, I thought it would only make you both unhappy to
hear it, and that is the reason why I never mentioned it. But
row, I must say, that I don't know, under heaven, how any-
one, barring him—the villain, and myself—could come to the
knowledge of what passed between us. There was nobody
present that I could see, and I don't think that he would be
apt to mention it to anybody, in regard that it would only
bring disgrace upon himself."

"Ha ! ha ! ma coleen," replied Patchy, "maybe you're a
little out there, anyhow Don't you know the little wind'y

that's in the back o' the kitchen, and that was then half open. Maybe there wasn't a certain *Baccach* peepin' in at the time, and that had both his eyes and his ears open to see and to hear all that passed; and maybe that same Baccach hadn't a bit o' goods about him that would have put daylight through the villain if he had laid an improper finger upon you."

As he spoke he pulled out an excellent case of pistols, and handed them round to the company.

"It wasn't for nothing," he added, "that I got the same wound that made me a cripple for life, in the wars against Cromwell, the villain, where I got a skelp of a bullet in the hip that has lamed me for life. Oh, we had plenty of Rappa- rees then, that did good service. Give me a glass o' whisky, till I drink their health; but mark me, I don't mane the Tories, although many people, in their ignorance, put them to- gether; for the Tories rob and murder the Catholics as well as the Protestants, whenever they could do it safely, the cowardly scoundrels. Thank you, Con M'Mahon. Here, then, is the health of the glorious Rapparees?"

He drank off the glass which old M'Mahon had handed him, after which the heroism of Rose—the fair Rose of Lis- boy—was next proposed, and, need we say, received with enthusiasm.

"Well," said Brian Callan, when this temporary excitement had settled down to something like sober conversation, "that I may never stir, Con M'Mahon, if you arn't the greatest schamer on the face of the airth; but sure we ought all to know you, you thief: sure it's as common as the church steeple that you can neither buy nor sell widout a joke.'

"Very well," replied the old hoaxer—for, in fact, he was such—"very well, then, a merry heart is always a light one: or, on the other hand, a light heart is always a merry one; and in truth, in my opinion, one laugh is worth fifty crys any day. And now that everything is settled, Brian, we'll be biddin' you and yours good night. The course of happiness is clear before the youngsters; and may God keep it so !"

There was one individual among them, however, who had paid a comparatively small degree of attention to the conversation which went forward. This person sat wrapped up, as it were, in himself, or in his exuberant imagination, watching an opening in the busy dialogues which intersected each other with such unbroken continuity. The person we allude to was the young Senachie, or story-teller, who now seeing that there was a lull in the conversation, as the neighbors were about to prepare for their departure, thought he might succeed in ar resting their attention for a short time, until he could disburthen himself of his legend.

"Con M'Mahon," said he, "I was goin' to tell them a story when you came in, but now that there's time to hear it, I'll go on wid it—hem ! There was a widow woman once, and she had three sons——"

"Owen, my boy," said M'Mahon, "I'm afraid its too late now to hear your story."

"Oh," replied Owen, "it's not a long one ; you'll be time enough—hem. There was a widow woman once, and she had three sons——"

"Some other time, Owen *abouchal*," said M'Mahon, with a grave but droll face; "on the night of the weddin', man alive ; keep it for the night o' the weddin'."

This jest of M'Mahon's produced, of course, an uproar of mirth, save and except on the part of the young couple, who kept considerably in the back ground. The strangers now took their departure, first having taken their *doch an durrush*, or parting cup, with the exception of *Patchy Baccach*, who was detained by Brian Callan for the night.

CHAPTER II

IT was usual, at the time in which the incidents of our story occurred, for the farmers of Ireland to allocate a place in the barns or other out-houses attached to their dwellings, in which their male servants, and sometimes their grown sons, should sleep. It was the custom then, and is, in many instances, to the present day. On the night in question, Brian Callan's young sons retired to the barn to sleep, accompanied by Patchy Baccach, who had a separate *shake-down* for himself. Young Owen, who was still full of his legend, and anxious to deliver himself of it, insisted on narrating it, but, as his brothers had heard it a hundred times, they preferred hearing Patchy's account of the wars—and to this Patchy readily assented. He amused them by many a wild account of those fierce and bloody conflicts, until both he and they fell unconsciously asleep.

In the meantime, Brian Callan and the other members of his family, after recommending themselves devoutly and piously to the protection of God, retired to their beds, and soon after were sunk in deep and dreamless repose. They all led innocent and inoffensive lives, were peaceful and industrious, and well beloved by their neighbors and acquaintances. With the exception of the robberies which, at that unsettled period, were so frequent, persons of their quiet character had nothing to fear; and, on this occasion, for reasons with which the reader will be made acquainted, Brian Callan and his family slept, in what they considered perfect security. In the dead hour of the night, however, a violent knocking took place at the door, and voices, marked by tones of turbulence and impatience, were heard outside. The family within immediately started up, and dressed themselves as hurriedly as they could. Rose, probably from a peculiar instinct of personal apprehension, was the first dressed, and, guided by that instinct, she immediately hid herself under a bed.

"Something tells me," she said, pale with consternation, "that this unlawful visit is made on my account, and that Lucas is at the head of it; but I will hide," she added, "and if it is me they want, say that I went to my aunt's in Dundalk, to spend a week or a fortnight with her."

She accordingly concealed herself under the bed, the only place of concealment which the house afforded. The other members of the family were in a dreadful state of terror They knew at once that those who were so violently and so vociferously demanding admittance were not the robbers by whom the country was then infested. The clang and jingling of their arms left no doubt of their being a military party; but, as Callan and his family were unconscious of having given any offense either to the law or government, so were they completely perplexed as to the cause of such an outrage Not that such scenes were then at all uncommon—far from it. The Tory-Hunting, as it was still called—as applied even to the Rapparees—was still going on in the country; and many a house was thus surrounded and searched by night, either from direct information that the family held concealed a Tory or a Rapparee, or from suspicion that they had done so, and a hope that they might find them there.

At length, a rather hoarse, stern voice said outside :

"Open the door, in the king's name. If you do not, we will break it in."

"What is your business with me or mine?" said Callan, from within "that you come to my peaceful house at such an unreasonable hour of the night. Why not come in day-light?"

"That is our own affair, and not yours," replied the same ruffian voice ; " but if you wish to hear it, be it known to you that we are come in search of a Rapparee, called *Patchy Baccach*, and we know him to be now with you. He is a setter for the Rapparees, and goes about as a lame beggar. Open at once, before we break in the door. You know now that we are upon the king's business ; and, as he spoke, he gave the door a heavy knock with the but-end of his carbine.

Callan, now perceiving that he had no alternative than that of yielding to their threats, opened the door, and admitted them. A candle was lit, and about a dozen men, in military uniform, at once entered the house, and after looking sharply about them, again demanded where the setter for the Rappa-rees was?

"You may believe me, as an honest man," replied Callan, "that the person you want isn't undher this roof. If he was, you would see him, for there's no place here where he could hide."

"That is more than we know," returned their leader, a stern, ruffianly-looking man, about forty-five years of age ; "but, in the meantime, we will search."

They accordingly commenced the search, and in a few min-utes pulled poor Rose, now less alarmed than she had been, from under the bed. Having heard that they were in pursuit of the Baccach—a circumstance very probable in the times of which we write—Rose felt considerably relieved, and contrived to say in a whisper to her mother, that there was no necessity for alarm on her account, and requested her not to make her-self at all uneasy.

"As for Patchy Baccach," said the leader, "it's a clear case that you have deceived us, and allowed him to escape

As it is, we must take this girl away with us until, you produce him. Such are our orders, and such is the law."

"Is it to drag my daughter out, from undher her father's roof, in the clouds of the night?" replied Callan, "an innocent child, that never gave offense to a human being. Surely, you have no king's authority for such an outrage as this—such a cowardly and unmanly outrage?"

"You had better keep a mannerly tongue in your head," replied the leader, whose name was Stinson; "otherwise it may be worse for you."

"I don't mane to offend you, sir," replied Callan. "I know what the law is about Rapparees, sure enough; but then, that is only in cases where the Rapparee or Tory is a relation of the family; but here there is nothing to justify your conduct, because I take God to witness that there is neither Tory nor Rapparee related, either by blood or marriage, to me, or any one belongin' to me. Don't, then, drag my innoffensive child from the protection of her family. Maybe you are a father yourself, and if you are, think—oh, think of what you'd feel to see a daughter of your own torn from your arms and from your heart; think of this, sir, and have mercy on us." And as he spoke, the bitter tears ran down his cheeks.

"It is out of my power, replied the man, quite unmoved; I have my orders, and I must obey them—let the young woman prepare to come along."

"Oh! no, sir," replied her mother, in accents of the most heart-rending entreaty, whilst the tears gushed from her eyes, "Oh! no; for the sake of the livin' God, no! Oh, if you have a wife, sir, or a daughter like her, as her father said to you, think how you'd feel if you saw that darlin' and beloved daughter torn away from her mother's arms at such an hour of the night, and by strange men—a girl that never in her life gave offense to man, woman, or child. Oh! have com-

passion upon us, sir; for, great God! she is our only daughter."

The stern miscreant, the instrument of a baser and far more
dishonorable man, merely returned the same reply as before;
when Rose, now in her mother's arms, said:

"I know, my dear mother, who the villain is that is at
the bottom of this; but don't fear for me. I have but one
life, and sooner than come to shame, I will lose it. *I am prepared.*"

"If one of the family is to go," said her father, still in tears,
"oh, take me, and leave our child to the mother that loves her
better than her own life I am ready to go with you—och,
do then take me, and leave the girl behind."

"No, but take me," added the mother, clasping her hands
in a state of the wildest distraction—"take me, and leave our
darlin' to the ould man, who will break his heart if she is separated from him."

"Not if he leaves her safe with you—safe in her own family," said her father, turning to his wife; "that's all I ask
And surely if you have a heart in your body," he added, addressing the leader, "a sowl to be saved, and a belief that God
is above you, and that you must account to Him for this black
outrage, you will spare her to her mother, and take me in her
place."

"I will take neither of you," said the man, "in the absence
of the Rapparee setter. She must come; for such are my
orders. If I was to consult my own will," he added, somewhat softened, "I would leave the young woman with you;
but that is out of the question. Prepare yourself, my girl—
you must come with us; and you need not be at all afraid—
there will be no harm done to you: so far from that, you will
be soon glad that we brought you to good fortune."

"Stop there," proceeded her mother; "I cannot see this—

I will not see my child destroyed when I can prevent it
Leave her with us, and we will give you up the *Baccach.*"

"Where is he?" said the sergeant.

"He's in the barn," she replied, "where the boys always
sleep."

"Go and arrest him forthwith," said Stinson, addressing
three or four of the men ; "but bring him with you by a different direction—you understand ! He musn't cross our path ;
for we know him. He hasn't Sarsfield at his back, now."

The barn in which the Baccach slept had, as most such
buildings have, two doors, for the purpose of winnowing corn,
by the strong draught of wind which they occasion. It is not
to be supposed that the noise and tumult about the house, and
the rattling of their arms, did not arouse and startle the inmates of the out-house. They were, in fact, awakened and
alarmed, and in an instant the Baccach was up, and in the act
of dressing himself with all the expedition in his power.

"I must be off," said he, throwing the straw upon which he
slept upon another heap that lay in the end of the barn ; "say
I went out early in the night, and that I wouldn't tell yez
where I was goin'. Blessed man, but it's I that could take
down a couple o' the villains, and would, too, only that it
would get the roof of every house belongin' to you burnt to
ashes, and you yourselves shot maybe, like dogs. But what I
fear most about is poor——" He paused, from a reluctance
to express the suspicions which pressed upon him, with respect
to their sister. "Now," he added, passing out of the back
door, "I'm off, and, thank God, the night's dark. Boult this
door, and if they come in, be sure to spake them fair ; otherwise you may get a dog's knock. As 'or me, I'm safe ; for
even if they caught me to-night, I would be at liberty to-morrow. I know that if they saw me, or met with me to-night,
they should take me to save appearances, and to have an ex

rase for bein' out, if any inquiry should be made about their
conduct In the meantime, I don't wish to meet them, bekase
I want to watch their motions, without givin' them raison to
suspect me. They call me Baccach ; but divil a many men iu
the county could cross a country with me for all that."

The truth is, that Patchy's lameness was but trifling, and
such as impeded his activity and speed only in a very slight
degree. Lame, however, he was, and that fact was sufficient
to fasten the nick-name upon him.

It is unnecessary to say that when the troopers came to
search the barn, they found that the hare had flown, nor did
this fact give them any uneasiness, inasmuch as his capture
was merely secondary to the great object of their visit.

"The scoundrel has disappeared," said the men on their return from the barn ; "but as he must have been aided and
abetted in his flight by this man's sons, we are, of course,
bound to take away the young woman, and keep her in close
imprisonment until he is produced."

"Such are our orders," replied Stinson ; "and you all know
that there is no discretion allowed to us in their execution.
Come, young woman !" he added, addressing Rose, and at the
same time laying his hand—gently, however—upon her shoulder, "you must accompany us, aud that without delay."

The wail and sorrow of the parents and of the two servant
maids cannot be described. Both parents clung to her, threw
their arms around her, and their grief was less the grief of ordinary sorrow than that of wild and hopeless despair. They
had heard of these matters before, when the relatives of proclaimed Tories and Rapparees were held responsible for their
appearance, under the penalty of transportation itself ; but
never yet had they heard of or known a case where an unoffending female, or a female at all, had been held accountable
for their capture or punished for their escape. Here the cases

did not tally. There was no parallel between them As the father said, there was neither Rapparee nor Tory connected with their family; and upon what principle, or with what object, their daughter should be dragged away from them in a spirit of such savage and licentious outrage, was a mystery which they could not fathom. The scene of separation was, indeed, a terrible one. It required both strength and violence to tear the parents from their child. As for Rose herself, although distracted and stunned by this sudden and unwonted violence, she was firm, and did everything in her power to console her bereaved parents. In fact, she felt not terror so much as resentment at this atrocious and cowardly outrage upon the peace and happiness of a family who had kept themselves aloof from the political convulsions of the times, and had, consequently, every claim to protection from the law. Her cheek mantled, and her eye flashed with indignation, but she knew that resistance and entreaty were both in vain, and, turning to her parents, she said, as she adjusted her cloak about her shoulders, addressing them:

"You both forget—we all forget—that there is a God above us, who can protect the innocent. Think of this, and take your daughter's word for it, that no man shall ever bring me to either guilt or shame while I have life in my body; but, in the meantime, I trust in the protection of the Almighty, who, should all human aid fail, is able to protect me When you see Con M'Mahon, tell him not to fear me; I will either live or die his: and I am sure that both he and you will do everything in your power to take me out of danger. In the meantime, don't be afraid; trust to God, and the intention that is in my own heart, should everything else fail me."

After one last heart-rending embrace they were then separated; and indeed it was evident from the silence and apparent reluctance even of those hardened veterans, that the task

which had been committed them was one from which their very
hearts revolted. Their leader, Stinson, took no personal part
in the separation of Rose from her parents. On the contrary,
his tough and indurated heart seemed to have been moved by
what had taken place before him, and his deportment, at first
rough and surly, changed by degrees into a mood that beto-
kened a sympathy which the nature of his duty rendered it
impossible, if not unsafe, for him either to exhibit by his manner, or to express in words. At all events, she was placed
behind Stinson, who, in order to prevent her brothers or any
of the family from dogging them on their way, placed a guard
both upon the dwelling-house and the out-houses, who remained
at their posts until all hope of discovering the route they had
taken became utterly impossible, after which they took their
way, and disappeared about a couple of hours before morning.

It is utterly impossible to describe the grief and distraction
of her miserable parents and family on that woful and unhappy night. After their feelings, however, had somewhat
subsided, or, we should rather say, when their very hearts had
become broken down and exhausted, her mother said, addressing her husband and the rest :

"Come, Brian, and all of you, our tears can do our darlin'
little good ; think of her own blessed words—*trust in the Almighty*. Since we cannot help her, then, any way else, let us
pray to that Almighty for her, and implore Him to protect
her innocence and her goodness from the snares that her enemies may lay for her, and to entreat that He may break down
their power over her, and disappoint their evil designs against
her ; for, poor girl, she has nobody now but that Almighty to
protect her."

They then knelt down to pray for her safety and preserva-
tion from all evil ; and, as they offered up those heart-felt and

agonizing prayers, it was pitiable to hear the deep groans
and irrepressible sobs by which they were accompanied. Toward morning, when the guards that had been left by Stinson, for the purposes already mentioned, had taken their de
parture, her brothers made their appearance in the house, and
on hearing that their sister was violently carried away, under circumstances so unaccountable and suspicious, their hearts were
at once rent by grief, apprehension, and indignation. What,
however, could the poor boys do? Indignation was vain,
grief was vain, and nothing remained but to await the return
of morning, in order to take such steps as might be deemed
most effectual for her recovery.

About nine or ten o'clock the next day, the melancholy
account of this daring and outrageous abduction had gone
abroad through the whole parish. The consternation, we need
scarcely say, was general, and the sympathy felt for this peaceful and unhappy family at once profound and active. Their
neighbors, friends, and acquaintances, all offered their services;
but, alas, what could be done? They had no trace of her, and
nothing to guide them but the fact that she had been taken
away by a military party, in consequence, as had been stated
by the leader of that party, of their having sheltered Patchy
Baccach, whom they denounced as a setter for the Rapparees,
and that she must be detained a prisoner until Patchy should
be given up to them. Whether Patchy was a setter for the
Rapparees or not, none of them could tell; but there were
persons among them who hinted that, if Patchy was a setter
for anybody, it was much more likely that he was a setter for
the military *against* the Rapparees; for that it was well
known he had been seen pretty frequently about the Armagh
barracks drinking and carousing with the soldiers. This certainly looked suspicious, especially when his visit to the house
of Brian Callan was connected with that of the military upon

the same night. Others, however, defended the Baccach, and said it was well known that he could deceive a saint.

"He goes among the sogers," they said, "to drink wid them, and then to pick out o' them where they've got ordhers to go next to take the Rapparees; and then he goes and puts the Rapparees on their guard—gives them the hard word."

While discussing this point, which we are not now about to determine, young Con M'Mahon entered the house, and immediately a pause occurred in the conversation. All eyes were turned upon him, and many persons, in a low voice, not intended for his ear, whispered: "God pity him! the Lord look down on him! but the poor boy is to be felt for this day, if ever a man was."

When Rose's lover entered his cheek was pale, but his eyes blazing. "What," said he, "what has happened? Can what I've heard be true? Is Rose gone?"

Her father seized his hand, and replied, with an emotion which almost deprived him of the power of utterance:

"She is gone, Con, she is gone; but where, for the present, we cannot tell. She was taken away by the sogers, and that's all we know about it; but, ahagur, there is no time to be lost. We must all set out and try to find some account of her. What do *you* intend to do?"

The young man paused, but on hearing the fact of her abduction confirmed, like her father, he was unable for some time to make any reply. A hot tear or two started to his eye, but he dashed them off, and seemed for a moment the very impersonation of vengeance. After a little, however, as if conscious of the necessity of coolness, he made an effort to become calm, and to a certain extent succeeded.

"Now," said he, "tell me all; tell me every word they said, and every thing that happened last night."

This the father did; and when M'Mahon had heard it all

he said, with another blaze of indignation; 'Come, Brian Callan, come with me to Armagh barracks. I think I know the villain that is at the bottom of this. Come, you and I only; who has such a right as her father, and the man that is betrothed to her? We *must* find her, I tell you—or if not, all the law in Europe—no, nor all the soldiers in Europe, won't save him from my vengeance. What is *my* life if *she* is gone! Nothing. I don't value it at one grain of chaff. Come, let us start."

"This is too much outspoken, Con," said her father. Don't talk as you do; you ought to know the enemies you may make by such language. I am sure the magistrates of the neighborhood won't overlook this outrage upon a peaceable and loyal subject. Let us apply to them, then, and I'm in hopes that they'll assist us, as it is their duty to do, and to throw light upon the misery that has come upon us."

"I hope they will," replied M'Mahon; "there are many of them good men; and, on the other hand, many of them persecutors. But, in the manetime, come with me straight to Armagh, to find out there whether any of the men have been abroad npon duty last night."

"Very well, replied her father   "In the name of God, let us go."

M'Mahon had come well mounted upon a stout horse to the house of his intended father-in-law, and in a few minutes the old man was in the saddle, and both set out for Armagh barracks. They reached there in a few hours, and, as M'Mahon's object was to see the Colonel of the regiment in which Lucas held his commission, they soon succeeded in procuring an interveiw with that gallant gentleman. His age was about sixty and his appearance that of a mild and benevolent man, as in fact he was. If he, had a fault at all as a military officer, it was an excess of indulgence to his subordinates whom he overlooked in many escapades, which, as they were not exactly connected with any breach of discipline or duty, and as peace now prevailed over the country, he looked upon them with rather a lenient eye. Notwithstanding this good-humored connivance at small offenses—which could scarcely be termed anything more, as they related to the profession, than semi-official at the most—yet was he known to be both stern and severe whenever any deliberate violation of duty was committed. He was a bachelor, and lived in a private house near the barracks : but as soon as he understood that Callan and M'Mahon wished to see him, they were immediately admitted.

"Well," said he, when they entered, "what is the matter? Have these d—d Rapparees been with you? Confound the scoundrels, they are harassing us to death in pursuit of them, but to no purpose. There is scarcely a day that we have not a party out after them ; and after all, we return as we went—no, faith, not as we went, but my men jaded and fatigued to death. I suppose you have been robbed?"

"I have, sir," replied Callan, "but not by the Rapparees."

"How is that?"

"On last night a party of soldiers came to my house, in the middle of the night, and took away my only daughter, by force and violence."

"By force and violence!" he exclaimed, starting—"a party of military take away your daughter by force and violence—impossible ; and in the king's name, too—more impossible still."

"It's truth, your honor,—too true it is, God help me ; and, what is more, we don't know where she is, nor where they brought her to."

The Colonel looked at the old man with astonishment, but at once perceived by his tears, and the deep affliction with which he spoke, that some gross or unusual outrage had been committed.

"Why, this," he said, "would seem almost incredible. Are you certain, poor man, that it was not the Rapparees who took her ?"

"Quite certain, sir ; they were troopers, in uniform, about a dozen or more of them. As for the Rapparees, it is a rule among them never to injure any woman, whether rich or poor, but rather to protect them. Their Captain would not allow it."

"Ah ! that Captain," exclaimed the other. "D—n the rascal ; many a long and fruitless chase he has led my poor fellows : however, we shall have him yet. In the meantime, tell me all about this business ; for, as it stands, I can make nothing of it."

The old man then related at full length, all the circumstances of the outrage, precisely as the reader is acquainted with them. When the Colonel heard him to the close, he paused for some time, but at length said·

"I am not surprised at your affliction, poor man. That law against Rapparees and Tories has not been acted on for some years. You say the lame rebel is not related to you ; and, in that case, I don't see why either you or yours should be held responsible for him."

"He is only a poor Baccach, your honor, who goes about begging from house to house for his bit—God help him !"

"Sir," said M'Mahon, who now spoke for the first time, "we came to you in ordher to know whether there was any party of your men out last night ; and we say, too, with too much truth, I'm afraid, that we have raison for suspectin' one of your own officers for bein' at the bottom of this villainy ; and if we find that he is, by the eter——"

The old man put his hand upon his mouth before he could

complete the oath. "Con, for God's sake, will you keep yourself quiet in his honor's presence. This young man, sir," he added, addressing the Colonel, "has a right to feel as much as any one livin' on this subject. He and my daughter were to be married in a couple of weeks"

"The officer's name I spake of, sir," persisted M'Mahon, but somewhat more calmly, "is Lucas; and we know that he tried to break down her virtue by a falsehood, and attempts at bribery, until he was near gettin' himself stabbed to the heart by her for his pains. You'll find, sir, upon inquiry, that the profligate had a party of your men out last night, and undher false pretenses, too."

Colonel Caterson—for such was his name—appeared at once to have been seriously impressed by the words which M'Mahon had just uttered. A new light seemed to break in upon him; and after reflecting in silence for a little, he at length said:

"Come, I was on my way to the barracks as you came in; et us go there. I shall inquire into this matter, and strictly, too."

On his arrival there, he immediately instituted the necessary inquiries, and especially whether Cornet Lucas had been out with any military party on the preceding night, to which he was answered directly and solemnly in the negative. Cornet Lucas himself, upon being sent for, appeared, and assured him upon his honor that he had not left his room during the whole night, as he could prove by several witnesses—which he did do—and, in fact, the unsuspecting Colonel discovered that not one of his men had been out beyond the hour usually appointed for their return to barracks.

"Now," said he, addressing Callan and M'Mahon, "you see I have made every necessary inquiry as to the cause of your trouble and suspicions. It is quite certain that no men from these barracks were at your house last night, nor had anything to do with the outrage committed against your daughter and your. family."

This intelligence was anything but agreeable ; and young M'Mahon, though forced to rest satisfied with it, maintained his opinion that the good-natured Colonel was imposed upon, and that Lucas had contrived to effect the abduction without his knowledge. This, indeed, was a very natural suspicion, if we reflect upon the loose and neglected state of discipline which prevailed in the British army at that period. Be this as it may, Callan and he were obliged to return home in such a state of sorrow and disappointment as may easily be conceived by our readers.

In the meantime, every effort was made for the recovery of the fair Rose of Lisbuy. Parties were out in all directions. The whole neighborhood—the whole parish—was canvassed and searched, but with the same melancholy result. Neither trace nor tidings of her could be found: The grief of her parents and family. was excessive—terrible ; and as for young M'Mahon, he was in a state of such absolute distraction, that his friends began to fear his reason would utterly abandon him. He could not rest—he could not partake of his ordinary meals ; but kept riding about from place to place in such a state of despair and apparent insanity, that he became the subject of general compassion.

On the night after the outrage, about the hour of eleven o'clock, he was on his return from one of those hopeless excursions, when he found himself challenged in a part of the road that was peculiarly solitary and lonely. Three men on horseback approached him, and one of them, in a full, rich, and mellow voice, after commanding him to stand, said :

"Sir, deliver your purse at the peril of your life.'

"Ah !" replied M'Mahon, " there are three to one against

me ; otherwise you should not have it without a struggle—nor even as it is, but that I am unarmed "

" Come," said the man who spoke, addressing the rest, " this fellow has spunk in him : here, take my pistols and cutlass, and retire, and by no means interrupt us. I will either teach the gentleman a lesson, or will learn one from him. Alight, sir ! I am now unarmed as you are, and if you prove yourself able to retain your purse, why, well and good—it shall be safe ; but if not, you must go home without it."

" It is a fair offer," replied M'Mahon, alighting, and I willingly accept it. Take it, then, if you can."

Now, before we proceed farther in the history of this exploit, we beg to inform our readers that young Con M'Mahon was one of the stoutest, most active, and courageous young fellows in the barony. In fact, there was no man in it who, in a personal contest, had any chance with him ; and,. besides, on this occasion, the loss of Rose Callan, and her mysterious abduction, had made him altogether desperate. At all events, the highwayman and he met, and in less than half a minute he felt himself, without receiving a single blow, stretched upon the road, the knees of the highwayman upon his body, and his throat within a gripe that he felt to be herculean.

" Do not strangle me," said M'Mahon ; " take my purse, and let me up."

" No," replied the other ; " I will not take your purse—I never took a purse in my life ; I always receive them with the consent of the donor. There now," he added, rising, " put your hand in your pocket, take out your purse, and hand it to me like a gentleman, saying : ' Sir, I present you with this, and I thank you for your forbearance.' "

" Here is my purse," replied M'Mahon, "and I must say, you deserve it ; for he is no common man who could have taken it as you did, and from me, too. It is not, however, my purse that is troubling me ; what is ten pounds to me, or tea thousand, in the affliction that is over me ?"

" Why," asked the highwayman, "what affliction is over you ?"

M'Mahou then related, with an emotion which he could not restrain, the calamity which befell his betrothed, under circum stances of such unprecedented outrage ; at the same time, swearing solemnly, that if Lucas proved to be the man, he would deliberately shoot him dead.

" Ha !" exclaimed the highwayman, " and so you suspect Lucas ; but there you are wrong. I have reason to know that *Lucas* is not the man ; however, the thing must be looked to. Stay where you are for a few minutes ; but, I beg your pardon, you have not told me your name."

M'Mahon then gave him a brief account of his name and family, after which, the highwayman paused for some time, and, having again desired him to keep his place for a little, he joined his companions, with whom he entered into consultation for a few minutes, after which they all returned and joined him.

" Now, M'Mahon," said the Rapparee, it so happens that I know your family well. There was a day when they were staunch friends to their unfortunate country, and sealed their affection for it with their blood."

" And would do so still," replied the young man, "if the occasion offered."

" I do not doubt it," replied the other ; " but the times are now changed, and, perhaps, so much the better. It is mad- ness to continue a losing and a hopeless game. I now return you your purse precisely as I received it from you. It is not upon you, or such as you, that I wish to exercise my office ; but upon those who are enemies to the liberty of my country. I like the courage with which you would have defended your property."

" I thought," replied M'Mahon, "that there was but one man who, upon equal ground, could have taken it from me."

"And it is, probably, well for you that *that* man is not here, or, perhaps, you would have gone home with lighter pockets. In the meantime, I shall see that man to night ; and, if I possess any influence over him—as I think I do—it will go hard if I don't prevail upon him to try and restore the fair girl, to whom you are betrothed, and perhaps inflict some punishment upon the villain who forced her away. The law is now all upon one side, and we must only endeavor to balance the account by availing ourselves of such opportunities against it as may offer, or as we can create by our wit and ingenuity. You may now go home in safety, and perhaps you shall hear from me ere long. If I succeed with *him*—of course, you know who I mean—there is a chance that your promised bride may be restored to you sooner than you imagine. This, however, if effected at all, must be upon the condition that you keep your adventure of this night a profound secret. You know the reward that is offered for the head of the *man* we allude to, and you know that spies are on the watch for him by night and day. His motions are consequently restricted, and any-thing that he may do in your business must be at the very risk of his life. Now, good night, and safe home to you !" And, having uttered these words, he and his party proceeded upon their way.

CHAPTER III

At the period of our narrative, there was no such body in Ireland as a constabulary or police of any kind, either to preserve the peace of the country, or to repress the local outrages which were continually breaking out in it. All this duty—and a harassing one it was—devolved upon the country magistrates and private gentlemen, aided by the military, who were called upon to discharge the duties of our present police, as well as those of soldiers. At this period, too, the country was overrun and ravaged by lawless bands of Rapparees, and the still more atrocious body of Tories, the latter of whom spared neither life nor property in their merciless depredations. With them religion, of which they were as ignorant as the brutes about them, was no safeguard whatever. The Catholic was robbed and slaughtered with as little remorse as the Protestant, whilst among the Rapparees, on the other hand, there was moderation and forbearance—the great and established principle on which they acted being, never to shed blood unless in defense of life, and under no circumstances to injure or maltreat any of the female sex, no matter what their rank or condition in life might be. The humanity of this regulation, however, was due to the celebrated individual who drew up the rules of their conduct, and by whose skill and ability they were organized and commanded. The discipline which he established was scarcely ever violated, and whenever it happened to be so, the offending party was severely punished, and in some cases handed over to the laws of the land. The reader may think this a strange and imprudent proceeding on the part of the Rapparees, as it might be naturally apprehended that such individuals would, as a matter of course, betray their accom plices to the government, from a principle of vengeance against them, as well as to secure their own pardon. This, however, is a mistake ; because the government had, from day to day, exact information regarding them, so that very little could be added to it, even by one of themselves. They shifted their positions perpetually, and scarcely ever remained twenty-four hours in the same place, so that the information of to-day was of no earthly use for to-morrow. The government of the day, besides, was rather imbecile, and although the Duke of Ormond issued many severe proclamations against them, containing offers of large rewards for the apprehension of their leader, yet for many a long year he could boast of but very slender success. Be this as it may, at the time we write of, whatever military forces lay in Ireland were scattered over the kingdom at large, in order to be able to check the outrages, and secure the depredators and murderers, if possible, wherever they appeared. The magistrates and other country gentlemen could not act either rigorously or safely without their aid, and hence their distribution, as we said, over the general surface of the country. For this reason, then, it so happened, that in the few barracks that were then to be found in Ireland, there generally remained but a small handful of men—just enough, as was calculated, to preserve the peace of the neighborhood. The reader will soon perceive why we allude to these facts, which are well known to every reader of Irish history to be correct and authentic.

When the party who took away Rose Callan left her father's house, they turned—after passing along the *boreen* which led to it, and on reaching the highway—toward the town or city of Armagh. The poor girl's distraction was indescribable, and her grief such as ought to have excited compassion in any heart in which lay a single spark of humanity. Indeed, it touched that of the man behind whom she sat.

"Oh, where," she said, as well as her sobbing would permit her, "where, in God's name, are you bringing me? Are you a man? Have you no compassion? You are a soldier, and ought to be brave; but surely no brave man would suffer himself to become an instrument in such a cruel and heartless outrage as this. Have you not the Rapparees and Tories to pursue; but what have either I or my family done that we should be treated as rebels and robbers? They are neither Rapparees nor Tories, but an innocent and inoffensive people, who conduct ourselves peaceably, and have never done or said anything against the government or the laws. As for the *Baccach,* we know nothing about him, except that he says he was at the siege of Limerick; but he is not a drop's blood to us, and why should we suffer fer him? We only help him, and give him an odd night's lodging, like any other poor man that's forced to beg his bit."

"God help you, my poor girl," replied the man, considerably softened, "it was not for the Baccach we came. That Baccach's a favorite in the barracks—and if I don't mistake, is a spy for the government against the Rapparees and Tories."

"He may be so," she replied, "and the greater villain he is for it."

"How?" said the man. "Is it for serving the government of the country? That is dangerous talk."

"Whether for the government or against it," she replied, " every spy is a villain, and none but a villain would be a spy for any party; but what do *I* care about that? I ask again where, in God's name, are you bringing me?"

"There is no use in telling you, my poor girl! I and those that are with me must do our duty."

"Duty!" she replied indignantly. "Do you cal dragging an unoffending girl, in the clouds of the night, away from her family, an act that comes within the duty of a soldier? If you be a man, you ought to blush for it. Why, what is the conduct of a spy to this? For God's sake, let me go home— say I escaped, and that you could not find me in the darkness. If you do, and that you come to my father's house, he will reward you well for it."

They had been at this time a little in advance of the rest of the party, and the dragoon to whom she spoke put his horse to an easier pace, and was about, as she thought, to make some reply to this proposal, when the others, whether from accident or design, trotted up and joined them.

"Sergeant," said one of them, "what do you stop for?"

"Why, to get my snuff-box," he replied, "and to have a pinch. I'm danged but my nose is lost for the want of one."

"Very well," replied the ruffian, "take it, and remember that we have a sharp look out behind you here."

They then proceeded, but he continued gradually to advance a little ahead of them, after which Rose heard him say, as if in soliloquy :

"No, no—it can't be done—I dare not risk it. My dear girl," he added, "do not talk to me—I feel that it is out of my power to assist you. All I can say is, put your trust in God ; but at the best it is a bad business, and I am sorry I had any hand in it."

"I am afraid," she replied, weeping bitterly, "that that is all that is left me—but it may be enough. I am innocent of any crime, and my faith in the Almighty is stronger than my fear of men ; besides, if the worst comes to the worst, it may be that I carry my own remedy as well as his punishment about me—that is, if my suspicions are right, as I fear they are."

In due time they reached Armagh, where, with the exception of two or three, they separated, and contrived to get into the barracks one at a time. That they were not challenged on entering the gate resulted from the fact that Lucas had contrived to place upon guard some of his own favorite men, who were his creatures on similar occasions.   In order to prevent all possibility of noise, Rose was hurried in between two men, one of whom tied a thick handkerchief over her mouth, in order to prevent her from crying out.   The outrage, indeed. was a daring one, and at a first view as foolishly and incautiously contrived as it was daring.   The fact, however, was, that the barracks at the time were nearly vacant, not more than one or two companies being then in occupation of them. The consequence was that Lucas, who knew that there were spare rooms enough in which to shut her up, had selected one in a remote position, and to which—as it and the others adjoining it were at the time uninhabited, though well furnished—he resolved to commit her, as being free from any in tercourse with the inmates of the place.   An old woman— confidential wretch of his—was prepared to attend upon her and under her guidance, and that of the two ruffians who had brought her into the barracks, she was hurried to the lonely room we have mentioned.   Here she found candles, a fire, and everything laid out for supper, not omitting two decanters of wine that stood upon the table.   By the time she entered the room, she felt herself nearly suffocated, and would have swoon ed for want of breath had she not—now that her hands were free—at once removed the handkerchief from her mouth Having done so she panted violently several times, until at length she found herself able to breathe without difficulty, upon which she looked at the old crone, and her first words were :

" Are you a woman ? have you the heart and feelings of a woman ?   Can you see such an outrage as this committed upon a young, inoffensive creatnre of your own sex ?   No ; I can't think it possible.   Oh, you surely will have compassion upon me.   I implore you, in the name of that God who is to judge you, tc pity me! Oh, enable me to escape from the villainy of this man. As you hope for mercy, enable me to escape! My father is a wealthy man, and will reward you well if you do."

The vile old creature gave a grin at first, by way of reply, out after a little she answered:

"Foolish girl, don't stand there crying and wringing your hands. What are you afraid of? Is it of one of the hand-somest young gentlemen in his majesty's service? Pity! troth I have neither pity nor compassion for you, nor the good fortune that's waiting for you. I only wish I was your age, and as handsome as you are, and maybe I wouldn't think my self the happy girl if I was in your place. Here now; take a glass of wine, and it will comfort you and put you in good spirits. What's father or mother to the like of such a beautiful young fellow as Cornet Lucas? Come, my pretty girl, take this glass of wine and it will cheer you."

There are some individuals—especially old women, when they happen to be wicked, as was the case here—upon whose features and whole person there is legible and visible to the most inexperienced eye, such an unquestionable and diabolical spirit of iniquity, that by one glance at them we are as capable of understanding their character as if being an acquaintance for years. The tones of her voice, too, afforded as strong and as undecided a proof of her depravity as did her features. Altogether, poor Rose felt that so far as the fiendish old wretch was concerned, there was no hope for her. She accordingly sat down on a chair, and maintained an unbroken silence to everything she said—a mode of proceeding which annoyed the vicious old crone to the quick. She felt that she was now treated with contempt, as well as with hatred and indignation. Respect for the taste of our readers prevents us from detailing the infamous tendency of her conversation, and the vile scope of her arguments, in attempting to undermine the pure principles of this virtuous and beautiful creature Rose, when she saw and felt the spirit of the female devil she had to deal with, never once opened her lips to her, as we have said. Neither did she now shed a tear. She saw there was a terrible trial before her, and her whole spirit was absorbed in its result. The girl was in despair, or very near it; but despair, even in cowards, has a courage that is often desperate: what, then, must it not be in a person who possesses strong natural courage, as was the case with her? Her tears, and the weakness which occasioned them, abandoned her; nay, her very fears, to a certain degree, left her, and she felt prepared, and almost anxious, for the coming trial, with a hope that it might end in her favor. Such, indeed, is true courage, especially when founded upon virtue and resolution; and shall we not add to this her strong confidence in the protection of God? At length the vicious old sibyl left her, and after having locked the door outside, Rose could hear her hated footsteps wending along the passage as she departed. Human nature is a strange mystery. Now that the wretch, bad as she was, had gone, Rose felt as if a portion of her strength and defense had departed with her. She did not think that any thing in the shape of her own sex could be aught but a protection to her; and the terror which she had partially subdued again returned upon her. The solitude of her position, and its remoteness from all human assistance, depressed her wofully. But again the thought of the Almighty, and a sense of his overruling providence, once more came to her support, and whilst in this state of mind she knelt down and prayed fervently to God, and with bitter tears of supplication besought his assistance. Having risen from her knees she looked around the room, and examined the windows, to try whether any mode of escape might present itself; but alas, the scrutiny was hopeless The windows were secured and immovable, so far as she could ascertain, and resisted all her attempts to open them. Finding the melancholy and hopeless nature of her imprisonment she sat down, and again her courage and resolution returned to her. It seemed that her situation resembled the horrors of some troubled dream, and once or twice she pressed her temples, looked at her hands, rose up and sat down again, with a hope that it might be one of those dreadful phantasms which sometimes persecute us in our sleep, and which we feel as a reality until we escape, and are relieved from them by awaking. These experiments satisfied her, however, that it was neither a dream nor an illusion, but a frightful and horrible truth. Whilst this awful agony wrought so terribly on her spirit, she heard the key of the door gently insinuating itself into the lock—she heard it turn—she heard the bolt shoot back, and the next moment Lucas entered the apartment. He immediately locked the door, and put the key in his pocket.

"My dear girl," said he, "what good angel brought you here? If I knew his name I would pray to him."

"A better angel, sir," she replied, "will take me, I trust, safe out of this."

"He must be a very good one, then, and a great deal stronger than me; for you are now in my power, and I would be glad to see the angel that would take you out of it. You repulsed me once successfully, but you will not do it a second time."

"Don't be too sure of that, sir," she replied; "keep your distance," for he was approaching her. "Sir," she added, "keep your distance. I wish I could address you as a gentleman and a soldier. I entreat you, sir, if you be either, to set me at liberty, and allow me to return in safety to my sorrowing and outraged family."

"I have not the slightest notion of it, I assure you," he re plied ; "but, listen, I would rather win you by love and affec tion than have recourse to violence."

"Violence ! you surely dare not have recourse to violence ; you know what the consequences must be to yourself. I en treat you, then, if you be either a gentleman or a soldier, to set me at liberty, and let me go home to my parents. They are not without friends who will bring you to an account for any violence you may dare to offer me. The Johnstons of the Fews are particular friends to my family. They are our landlords ; and you may believe me when I tell you, that if you even attempt to insult or injure me, they will bring you to a short and sharp account for it."

The knowledge of this fact staggered the young villain for a few moments, and he seemed to pause for a while and be come thoughtful. While he is thinking, we will say a few words about that once remarkable family. The Johnstons of the Fews, then, were the most celebrated and active men of their day as Tory hunters, and had won a reputation as ex tensive as the kingdom itself, for pursuing, capturing, and bringing to justice those unprincipled banditti who robbed and murdered in all directions, and kept the whole country in a state of terror and ferment. The activity, courage, and perseverance of this family were astonishing ; and, in truth, both the country and the government were under great obli gations to them. They were also strong, but open opponents to persons of the Catholic creed ; but their principles as land lords were decidedly feudal. Of course, they had a vast num· ber of Roman Catholic tenantry under them, and although they proclaimed themselves bitter enemies to the Church of Rome and her adherents, yet, as the Catholics on their pro perty were *their* Catholics, woe betide the man—no matter what his rank or condition might be—who happened to offend or injure any one of them. The consequence was, that their violence was looked upon, especially by the Catholics of the day, as "full of sound and fury, signifying nothing ;" and if any person of that religion living on their property felt aggrieved, the first individual of might or rank to whom they applied was certain to be some one of the "Johnstons of the Fews."

Our readers will now understand the force of Rose's argument, when she pleaded their relation as landlords to her family.

" Well," said he, " let the Johnstons of the Fews rest—there is no one going to interfere with them ; but, in the meantime, I don't see why I should not prove myself a hospitable Irishman—why I should not shake hands with my beautiful guest, and welcome her to the place I have provided for her. Thero is no harm in that, I hope. I mean it all in love and affection."

As he spoke he was again approaching her.

" Stand back, sir" she replied, quickly and resolutely drawing an Irish skean, or dagger, out of her bosom. " There's only two lives between us ; advance another step and one of them will be taken. Give up your villainous design at once, for if you approach another step, I will plunge this skean into your body, and if I fail in that, I will plunge it into my own; so that, in whatever way it may end, you will lose your object. Stand back, then ; for, as God who sees my heart and knows my determination, I will keep my word. In whatever way it may end, this will be a black night to you."

" You know," said he, " I might bring in assistance. and have you disarmed. You know that ; so you may as well throw your skean aside, for I will do it."

" You may," she replied ; " but the first glimpse I catch of any assistance coming with you, that moment will I stab myself to the heart. In any sense, in every sense, I defy you

4

then ; and besides, I trust in the protection of God, who is stronger than you and all your wicked instruments."

"Very well," he replied, "I shall take another course. Be assured I shall subdue you yet, although I would rather do it by kindness and affection, as I have said, than otherwise. Did you never hear of such a thing as ' starving the garrison ?' "

"I have some notion of what you mean," she returned : "but, even so, I have my own remedy, thank God, and will use it sooner than ever you should gain your vile and cowardly purpose."

"Very well," said he, "we shall see the upshot. As I have life, I shall starve you here until you will not be able to use your dagger. I now leave you, and remember that you will find my words prophetic and true."

" And so shall you mine," she replied ; "but think of the consequences of this conduct—what will they be to you? It cannot pass without discovery, and when it is known you will be dragged to disgrace and punishment. You will die a shameful death, if you persevere in your wickedness."

"I leave you now," said he ; "but out of my hands you never shall escape until you are subdued and overcome."

"I have told you before," she replied, "that it cannot be. You are bringing your own fate upon your own head."

"Time will tell," said he ; "but I now leave you."

He accordingly withdrew, locking the door after him ; and in a few minutes the old crone returned, and, without uttering a syllable, carried off with her every particle of food and every drop of drink that was in the room, with the exception of one decanter of wine. She locked the door as before, and poor Rose was left in solitude and silence, in such a state of mind as it is not necessary for us to describe to our readers.

She was a brave and great girl ; but there are hundreds of thousands as brave and as great throughout the respectable peasant homesteads of our country. Whilst Lucas was in conversation with her, and indeed so long as he remained in the room, her beautiful form seemed, as it were, transfigured into the very spirit of resolution and courage ; her cheeks and temples glowed with the determined purpose of her heart, and her beautiful eyes flashed with a fire that shot from them like lightning, and gave unquestionable proof that the dreadful resolution she had threatened she would most assuredly exe- cute.

On that night, Patchy the Baccach—whom our readers, we presume, may already suspect of playing a double game be- tween the Rapparees and the military—came to the resolution of discovering, if possible, the place of concealment to which the unfortunate girl might be committed. With this intention he crossed the country toward Armagh, which he reached some short time previous to the arrival of the party. He had been permitted to sleep occasionally in some unoccupied lum- ber-room in the barracks, and, not unfrequently, was allowed to spend his nights in the guard-room, where he amused the men with wonderful narratives of his adventures while in the Irish army. The soldiers knew that he was under the protec- tion and in the confidence of the officers, and on this account he was admitted freely, and at all hours. On the night in question he presented himself, and was received with that good-humored but contemtptuous banter, to which he was well accustomed, and to which he always replied with very amusing drollery.

"Well, Patchy, what good news to-night, you lame old rebel ?"

"Why," replied Patchy, "do you call me an ould rebel ? I look oulder than I am, I know ; but maybe if you were afther harrowing all that I ploughed, you'd have three wrinkles in your face for my one. Ould ! a man at forty-two is only in his prime of life, and if it were not for this lameness, I'd tache some of you what activity manes. Sure, I often danced a hornpipe upon a soap-bubble widout ever breakin' it. Mav rone! but I was nearly *cotch* by the same lameness though. the night the bloody Rapparees gave me the chivvy-chase. To think of the villains followin' me to within a hundred yards of the barracks!"

"The ground must have swallowed them, then, Patchy; for when we turned out to pursue them, there wasn't a man of the scoundrels to be found."

"But sure, they say their Captain can make himself invisible whenever he likes, and that he carries bracken seed about him. for the very purpose."

"Faith, and they must all have carried it about them or that night; for devil a man of them was visible at all. Well but have you no news in particular to-night?"

"Troth, *some*," he replied, significantly, "has *good* news to night, and some has but indifferent. I missed my *set* this time at the Raps; but you know the worse luck now, the better again. It'll go hard wid me or I'll have them yet especially the Captain. Och, I'm tired and starved, and must go and throw myself on some shake-down in the ould lumber room."

Instead of going to the lumber-room, however, he kept dodging about the barracks until the troopers arrived, wher he planted himself opposite the windows in order to reconnoitre their proceedings, and to ascertain, if possible, how they might dispose of the unhappy girl, in whose fate he felt deeply and intensely interested.

"I will watch the windows," thought he, "and who knows but I may find out where they will place her. That's all I want: for I know the man that will take her out of the heart's blood of the barracks, if he only knows where to find her.'

The night was fortunately very dark, and he kept walking up and down opposite the windows. He felt no surprise on seeing Lucas's room lighted—for he was well aware of its position—but on seeing another apartment in a remote part of the building, which he knew to have been, until that night, unoccupied for a considerable time past, he began to entertain a strong suspicion that it might be that which they had selected as her place of captivity—at least until her ruin should be accomplished. Here he remained until Rose had been left to herself, and from this position he observed her attempting to ascertain if any kind of escape were available by the windows. In making the experiment she had placed the candle on the window-ledge, so that he had such a distinct view of her as at once satisfied him of her identity and the place of her imprisonment. To communicate with her, however, without the risk of discovery, he felt to be out of the question; but he thanked God that he had at least ascertained the locality of the room in which they had immured her; and to prevent any possibility of mistake, he reckoned the windows from the forth point of the range, until he came to that of the apartment which contained her, and placed a mark of three round stones close to the wall directly beneath it, lest there might be any mistake in his reckoning. Having accomplished so much, he felt that to leave the barracks at that unseasonable hour, after having so recently returned to them, might occasion suspicion. He accordingly retired to the lumber-room already mentioned, which was his usual place of rest when among the military ; and as he really felt much fatigued after his difficult and harassing journey across the country, he soon sank into a sleep, at once deep and refreshing. The next morning he awoke late, but active and recruited in strength. Having dressed himself— if we may say so, considering the habiliments he wore--he joined one of the soldiers' messes, where he amused them, and breakfasted besides to his heart's content. He then prepared to leave the barracks, but on his way was met by Cornet Lucas.

"Well, Patchy," said that gentleman, "how the devil does it happen that you are in barracks this morning?"

"Faith, for my own safety, your honor," replied Patchy; "but how the devil did it happen that you ordhered me to go to Brian Callan's last night, where a party of your men came to take me prisouer as a spy to the Rapparees? Doesu't your honor know the hunt they give me about a month ago, almost to the very gate of the barracks, and that mortal man never had such an escape as I had?"

"What party, Patchy? No party from these barracks was out last night. I believe you know all the men here, and you cau say whether any of them was at Callan's."

"Faith, I can say no such thing," replied Patchy, "for the best raison in the world, bekase I didn't see them."

"You didn't see them? That is unfortunate. How did it happen that you didn't see them?"

"Why, sir, bekase when I heard they were lookin' for me, I tuck to my scrapers."

"Did they commit any outrage?"

"Not, sir, that I am aware of, barrin' drivin' me out of my warm bed, the thieves, when I was tould they were lookin' for me."

"Patchy, my man, I never thought you a blockhead until now. Don't you understand it?"

"The devil a bit, your honor; it's Greek to me so far."

"Why, Patchy, the villains must have been the Rapparees. You know yourself they're not over head and ears in love with you."

"Faith, you've *hot* it there, sir—nor with your honor, either," replied Patchy; "but what I wish to know is, why you sent me there last night, sir?"

"Simply, Patchy, to bring about what has happened. I now know the Rapparees are in this immediate part of the country. They must have seen you goin' to Callan's, and your presence there it was which occasioned their midnight visit to his house. I hope they offered no violence to his family," he added, keenly scrutinizing Patchy's countenance as he spoke. "They say their Captain is in love with Miss Callan."

"That may be, sir; but it's the first time I ever heard of it; but why did you send me to where I stood a hundred chances to one of falling into their hands? Don't you know, sir, they're on the look-out for me night and day; and besides, by sendin' me there, you prevented me from makin' good my set upon them. But why did you send me at all, sir?"

"Why, to satisfy myself that they are in the neighborhood: and besides I depended upon your own ingenuity in escaping them. You see I was right; but I wish you had seen them, that you might give me some account of their personal appearance."

"Personal appearance, inagh (forsooth). Why, doesn't your honor know they never appear the same thing two days runnin', or rather two nights runnin'; and as for their Captain, he can change himself in such a way—face, dress, discourse, and all—that his own men often doesn't know him from Adam."

"So they say, indeed. In the meantime, I hope they have offered no violence to Callan's family. Yes, you are right, Patchy, for it is well known that they sometimes assume the uniform of his Majesty's British soldiers, and commit the most atrocious depredations in their name. It is very probable that if they committed any outrage upon poor Callan's family last night, they had recourse to the same disguises. Now, go and try your hand at tracing their whereabouts. It is clear that they are in the neighborhood. You know the reward that is offered by the Government for their leader, and that if **you** enable us to secure *him*, you will get an ample share of it."

" Isn't that what I'm thinkin' of, sir, day and night ; but, to tell you the truth, the people—I mane the Catholics, your honor—are beginnin', I think, to suspect me ; and if it 'ud be agreeable to you, sir, to give me a few lines from undher your own hand, by way of probation, jist to recommend all loyal subjects to prevent me, as far as they can, from receivin' any injury from the rebelly Papists, it would be of great use to me. About a fortnight ago I met one of those terrible men, the Johnstons of the Fews, and he was very near sendin' me to jail as a rebel that had fought against King William at the Boyne and the siege of Limerick, and only I referred him to Colonel Caterson, he would have done it. I'm not safe, sir, from either party, I tell you, without some such protection."

" Very well, Patchy ; stay where you are for a few minutes, and I will return with the document you want. It may serve you, certainly—at least with the magistrates and the loyal portion of the community—and you shall have it. In the meantime, don't conceal any outrage that the Rapparees may have committed last night from the people ; that is, if they have committed any, which I hope they did not."

In a few minutes he returned with the following document, which he presented to Patchy, who, after having received it, immediately left the barracks. It was to the following effect :

"This is to certify, that the bearer, Patchy M'Quade, commonly called Patchy Baccach, is a loyal subject, and considered worthy the protection of the garrison of Armagh, and all other loyal men in this His Majesty's kingdom of Ireland.

"(Signed)   WILLIAM LUCAS,

"Cornet in His Majesty's Third Dragoons."

Patchy, who was no scholar, put the paper carefully in an inside pocket, feeling perfectly aware that its discovery upon him by those of his own creed, who were ignorant of his peculiar position between the Rapparees and the military, might look upon him as a spy for the Government—a character which, at that time, was attended with anything but security He was possessed, however, of great cunning and ingenuity, and the reader will soon see the purpose to which he applied this document, and his object in procuring it.

CHAPTER IV.

PATCHY's connection with the Rapparees was closer and more confidential than our readers have yet been enabled to guess at. The duties which he discharged toward them were various and important. In the first place, from the trust which was placed in him by the military, he always became ac quainted with the projected movements of every party whc upon any information received as to their places of conceal ment, had been appointed to capture them. In consequence of this knowledge on his part, he was always able, by dis patching some trustworthy scout to their place of rendezvous for the time being, to anticipate and defeat the movements of the military. Again, he acted as a *setter* for them, which he did by traversing the country and ferreting out such circum stances as enabled him to mark the houses of persons who were known to be in possession of large sums of money, plate, and other valuables. In such cases, he contrived to examine the peculiar structure of the buildings, their strongest and weakest points of defense, together with the number and de scription of arms that were kept for the safety of their pro perty. If he could tamper with and corrupt a servant, it was so much gained; and the latter was always certain to receive a portion of the plunder. Again, he acted as a poacher, in which capacity he procured considerable quantities of ammuni tion powder, through the officers of the barracks, to whom he disposed of the game, declining, in most cases, to receive any thing but powder for it. In order to prevent suspicion, he assured them that he was the worst shot, as a sportsman, that ever leveled a gun; that for one hare, or partridge, or grouse he brought down, he missed twenty, and that it was a sin and a shame to think of the loads of powder he wasted. This custom of military officers exchanging powder for game supplied by poachers at their barracks, or other stations, has been practiced within our own memory, and to our own knowledge. In addition to all this, worthy Patchy frequently hung about public inns, ale-houses, and other places of entertainment, especially for travelers and wayfarers, into whose circumstances and motions he pried with equal success and ability. On these occasions he was always accompanied by a smart, active lad, who passed for his son, and to whom was intrusted the task of communicating to the nearest rendezvous of the Rapparees the intelligence he had gained.

Such is an accurate description of the character of Patchy Baccach, who, although he took no part in the actual robberies and other outrages perpetrated by the Rapparees, was yet one of the most useful and accomplished vagabonds among them. He always knew their haunts, even for a week or fortnight to come, unless when some information against them, or an occasional pursuit by the military, occasioned them to make a sudden change in the plan of their operations.

At the period of which we write—toward the close of King Charles the Second's reign—Ireland was covered with a vast quantity of wood and forest, which has altogether disappeared. The roads, too, were bad and few in number. In general they were paved with large, broad, solid stones, somewhat greater in size than a quartern loaf ; and what was still more extraordinary, the principle of selecting the most perfect level was either then unknown, or purposely disregarded. It has been asserted, but with what truth we will not undertake to say, that they were run "up one hill, and down another," in order that the traveler—at a time when the country swarmed with the wildest and most ferocious banditti, murderers, wood-kerns, and other licentious profligates of the period—might have an op portunity of surveying the road before him, and the country about him, to ascertain from this point of elevation what the prospects of danger, or the chances of flight and safety might be. This argument, however, is of a piece with the skill and wisdom which constructed such roads. At all events, be the roads as they might, there is no doubt that the surface of Ireland at that time was extensively covered with many thick and dense forests which no longer exist—a circumstance which accounts for the difficulty of capturing those Tories and Rapparees, as well as for the long reign of terror which they inflicted on the country. Be this as it may, Patchy directed his steps towards *the* Newry,·as it was then called, and having arrived at a farmer's house not far from the road, he resolved to claim the hospitality of the family, and remain there until dusk. He accordingly entered the house, which was rather a comfortable one, but found only a middle-aged woman and a couple of little girls within. The woman was in tears, and seemed full of sorrow, but the children were evidently too young to understand the cause of her grief. She sat upon a chair at the far side of the fireplace, having her apron thrown over her left shoulder, and her face toward the door. In this position she rocked herself to and fro, as is the custom of Irishwomen when in a state of affliction, and every now and then she sobbed and wiped her eyes with the apron, which she had thus disposed for the purpose.

"Daicent woman," said Patchy, "what's the matther wid you that you seem in sich affliction? I hope you have lost none of your family? But, even if you have, you know it's the fate of nature, and we must submit."

"Loss!" she replied. "Oh, thin, it's we that had the bitther loss—three of the best friends we ever had."

"Chiernah!" exclaimed Patchy, "*three* is it? Why, God he knows, a body 'ud think that one ought to be enough."

" Aye, and one too mnch, too," she said ; " but I tould Darby that it would be so ; but in ordher to save the beg-garly penny, see what he has brought on us—' save a shillin' and lose a pound ;' for so it was in this case at any rate."

" But how is it ?" asked Patchy. " What part of your fam-ily did you lose, honest woman ?"

" Oh, then, three o' the best cows that ever went into byre. They're gone, and we'll never see hilt or hair of them ; and now we'll have nothing for it bnt the black wather to kitchen our bit, let alone the loss of the butther that we had to make up the rent. Wurra, wnrra, what'll become of us ?"

" Faith, good woman," replied Patchy, " that's a bad bnsi-ness ; and who do you suspect for them ? Who do you think took them ?"

" Who ?" she replied ; " why, who but the Rapparees ?"

" The Rapparees ! faith and yon must have given them offense some way ; bekase it's a rare thing for them to come down upon the likes o' you so severely as that. It's the rich Prodestants that they always harry. I tell yon then to your face, that you must have provoked them some way, or they'd never lay a finger upon either you or yours."

" It wasn't my fault," she replied ; " I argued strongly with Darby abont it ; bnt when that terrible Captain of theirs was laid up a cripple—havin' lost the use of his limbs—Darby thought he'd never recover, and that he might sknlk out of his bargain wid him."

" What bargain was that ?"

" Why you see, the Rapparee entered into an agreement with the people of the country, especially the farmers, that if they'd pay him so much a year he'd undertake to keep them harmless. If they lost cattle or any other property he bound himself either to recover it for them, or make up the loss from his own pocket. In the meantime, while he was ill and a

helpless cripple, the devil tempted Darby, whose heart is too
much in the arraghids (money), to break his agreement, and
keep back what he promised to pay yearly for his protection."

"Phew!" exclaimed Patchy: "then you may whistle for
your cows. Devil resave the hair o' them ever you'll see
Your nagerly husband, thinkin' the Captain 'ud never recover,
and knowin' besides that he was ill and in want, went and de-
sarted him in the day of his trouble; but now he is well, and
has twiist the power over the country he ever had, and the
devil a man that ever broke his agreement wid him, when in
the day of his distress, but will sup sorrow for his conduct,
and the devil pity every treacherous and beggarly rascal that
did so. They say it was few that did it, and so much the
betther for them that was honest and faithful to him; but
woe betide the nagers that treated him as your beggarly
scoundrel of a husband did. Devil a thing I heard this
month o' Sundays that has pleased me more than the loss of
the same cows; but, in the manetime, I didn't care if I had
something to ait. There's a vacancy in my stomach that's
anything but agreeable or pleasant, and I don't care how soon
it was filled up."

"Well, honest man," replied the woman, "although you
don't seem to feel much compassion for our loss, still, they say,
it's our duty to return good for evil; so if I have time to toss
you up a rasher before Darby comes in, I will; but if he
catches you at it, the house won't hould him. Whisper, ac-
cushla! he's a miser and a skrew, and I believe in my sowl
that if his salvation was on the one hand, and a brass farden
on the other, wid his choice of either, he'd secure the brass
farden."

"God help you wid him, poor woman!" exclaimed Patchy;
"it was a black day you ever seen the *keout*; but still an

all, get us the rasher, and we'll bear the consequence if he comes."

The timid but good-natured woman prepared the rasher with all possible expedition, and Patchy was just si.ting down to do it ample justice, when in walks the miser himself, with a small, withered face, and sharp, piercing, little eyes, in which gleamed an expression of fierceness and distraction, resulting from the loss he had sustained, and his evident want of success in finding any trace or intelligence of his cattle. He first fastened an angry glance upon Patchy, and then upon his wife.

"What's this, Peggy?" said he; "is it wastin' my hard-earned substance in this manner you are, upon such a lame runagate as this? *Dhamno orth!* (damnation on you) do you think I can stand by and look at sich extravagance as this, especially as I'm fairly starved wid hunger myself. Be-gone out o' this, you devil's *lomenther* (a lame person); I must have my dinner." And as he spoke he was about to seize the wooden trencher—for delph was almost unknown among the farmers of that remote period—upon which Patchy's rashers were smoking.

"Aisy, my good neighbor," said Patchy, gripping it firmly; "will you make a wager?"

"A wager! What wager? No, I won't."

"Bekase," proceeded Patchy, "I'll hould fifty to one, and that's long odds, that a morsel of that same rasher will never pass between your yellow tusks; and I'll double that again, that if you don't sit down there and behave yourself like a quiet, daicent, and hospitable man, as you are *not*, I'll show you three inches of your own tongue, by way of novelty and amusement to yourself. So keep a *calm sugh*, my ould codger, until I finish my male's mait. Do you understand any thing by that?"

The old miser sat down, and, placing his withered face upon his withered palms, sighed and groaned as if his very heart would break.

"Ay l" he exclaimed, "robbed, every way robbed—first by a foolish wife, and again by these thieving Rapparees. Oh, my three beautiful cows : the likes o' them wasn't in the parish, iu the county, in the kingdom, and the landlord coming down on us for the rent. Oh, *chiernah*, what'll become of us? It's it that's the black business."

In the meantime, honest Patchy was bolting the rashers with a humorous expression of countenance, which was irresistible when contrasted with the vindictive glare which the miser from time to time turned upon him. Whenever he caught the old fellow's eye, he gave him a comic wink and a nod which, in the state of his mind at the time, nearly drove him furious.

"Well," said he, "what's this your name is ?—Darby, Darby Soolaghan. Well, Darby, upon my reputaytion as an honest man, I have *ett* many a good rasher in my day, but the likes of this never went down the red lane (throat) ; and it's h. ck and grace your daicent woman of a wife will have for helpi ig the poor Baccach to these two pounds of it, not forgetting ne fine farral of *arran* (bread) that she put along wid it. J id you rear and feed the pigs yourself, Darby ?"

"Carry on," replied Darby, looking furiously at the wi'e ; "carry on, but she'll hear of it."

"Well now," said Patchy, who had nearly dispatched the rasher, "weren't you a penurious old scoundrel—ay, and a hard-hearted one to boot—to take advantage of the Captain's illness, and refuse to pay your engagement to him ? I now ax you a question : Is this the first time your cattle were taken from you ? Answer me the truth."

"Well, no, it is not ; but anyhow I'll never see them again,

I know, and then we're ruined. But this is Shane Bearnah's doin's ; he's as great a thief of cows and horses as Cahir na Cappul himself, oh chiernah !"

"*Dhomno orth*, you yellow disciple, will you give over grun:in' and groanin'," exclaimed Patchy ; "answer me directly. Is this the second time your cows were taken ?"

"It is. Blessed Father, what *will* become of us ?"

"And when they were taken first, did you get them back ?"

"I did, I did ; bekase I then paid my agreement."

"Then the Captain kept *his* word wid *you* ?"

"He did, indeed ; when he heerd of it, they were back with me in forty-eight hours."

"And you broke *your* word wid *him*—refused to stand by him when he was sick, and not able to act for himself. The devil's cure to you, then, and that's my compassion for you. You skamin' ould sinner, do you think I don't know you well ? Doesn't the wide world know you, and that you're as great a scrub as your wife's a daicent woman ? Why didn't you pay what you promised to pay ? Answer me that !"

"I hadn't it ; I couldn't afford it."

"That's a lie, Darby ; every one knows you're wealthy, and how you get your wealth, by sellin' out provisions on dear summers at three prices to the poor ; but listen —pay me up your arrears to the Captain before I lave the house, and, although I never laid my eyes upon him or one of his men, I'll undertake, through my acquaintance wid a relation of his, that your cows will be in your own byre widin a few days at least ; and this I engage not for *your* sake, but for the sake of your daicent, kind-hearted wife, and your innocent childer there. How many have you of them, Mrs. Soolaghan ?" he inquired from the good woman.

"Troth, nine o' them ! but there's none in the house at

present barrin these two little girleens ; the rest, poor things
is all hunting afther the cows."

"There's no use in that," replied Patchy. "If Shane
Bearnah * has got them, no one but the Captain can have
them brought back to you. However, pay attention to
what I have said, and maybe it'll be betther for you
all."

"That is, give away a sartinty for an unsartinty. I'm not
the fool to do it," replied Darby. "What do *you* know
about them ? Ay, indeed, give my money to you, a vagabone
lomenther, that may never show his face to us again. Oh,
catch me at it !"

A long altereation took place between him and his wife,
who, aided by Patchy, at length succeeded in prevailing upon
him to intrust the arrears of his *black mail* to the latter, who
having secured it in his pocket, said with a grin :

---

* Shane Bearnah was one of the chief men in the great Rapparee's
gang. His department was the stealing of cows and horses, and every
description of the more important domestic animals ; but, indeed, his
thefts were principally confined to the former, as being the most lu-
crative, and the more easily conveyed from one part of the kingdom
to another. He was second only, as a thief of this description, to the
celebrated Cahir na Cappul, or Charles Dempsey, who was born near
Ballybrittas, in the Queen's County. Shane Bearnah has no distinct
biography, as Cahir na Cappul (Charles of the Horses) has ; but his local
celebrity, and the traditions of his exploits in various parts of the North
of Ireland, are perhaps equal to those of his great rival and contemporary. Caves, and isolated spots of green pasture, in the recesses of
some of the Northern mountains, are still pointed out as *Shane Bearnah's Stables,* or, in other words, as the localities in which he used to
conceal his stolen horses. One of them is to be found in that long
range called the Slieboen Mountains, which separate a portion of Ty-
rone and Monaghan from each other. It is said of Shane Bearnah,
that he was born without teeth ; but that he could, notwithstanding
the want of them, bite a piece out of a thin plate of iron with a
little difficulty as if it had been gingerbread.

"Now, you devil's limb of a miser, how do you know whether you'll ever lay eye on either cows or money again?"

"I'll hunt you through the kingdom, or I will," replied Darby, perfectly appalled at the threat. "I'll send the sogers afther you, and swear that your'e a Rapparee in disguise."

"Well, you ould sinner," said Patchy, "for the sake of your wife and family, I'll do what I can for you; but it's now between the two lights,* and I must be goin'. In the manetime, thank you, Mrs. Soolaghan, for your kindness to the poor Baccach. I hope you'll have no occasion to be sorry for it. Good-bye, ma'am, and good-bye to you, you ungrateful ould schamer; maybe I'll do betther for you than you desarve."

"For God's sake do," replied the wife; "for if you have betrayed us or taken us in, little you know the life I'll lead on account of it."

Patchy then took his leave of them, and departed on his more important mission.

The night set in very dark, and Patchy resumed his journey along the road, which at that time led by a rather circuitous road to the town of Newry. Having gone forward a few miles, he struck off the highway by one of those old unfrequented paths, which the slight improvements in roadmaking that were even then beginning to appear, had caused to be abandoned. There were few houses, as he proceeded, around or near him; the country was very much covered with wood, and had altogether, even in daylight, a solitary and desolate aspect. The wild and rugged outline of the old road, now choked up, as it was, by weeds, and almost covered with rank grass and brambles, was, however, quite familiar to him, and he advanced into the lonely region before h m with more ease and speed than might have been expected. We should have said that a portion of the ground through which this ran, had

* A common expression for twilight

been recently cultivated, so that, in point of fact, it was impossible for a stranger to imagine for a moment that a road, no matter how rude, had ever traversed that direction at all. It was no easy task, then, to know from what part of the new highway the turn across the fields toward it should be made, especially at night. To a stranger the matter was an im possibility, for in consequence of the district through which it ran having been scarcely ever inhabited, the very recollection of it had been nearly forgotten. In the meantime Patchy struggled on, not certainly without a good deal of difficulty, until he had advanced about four miles, when the wood became denser, and the path more indistinct and difficult. He now knew that he had not much farther to go, and after losing some time in searching about, he came upon a rope, by which, through many intricate and apparently inaccessible passages, he was enabled to reach a thick and impervious mass of underwood, so closely woven together, that it took some minutes to find the private passage. Having found it, he went on, slightly stooping until he reached a large clump of immense fern, through which he made his way by putting it aside with his hands. Immediately behind this was an opening to a cavern, into which he at once entered. He now knew his position, and proceeded accordingly. Having advanced about ten yards or so, he turned by a sharp angle that led to the right, and having followed this about six or eight yards more, he found it diverged to the left, when he saw a dim light in the distance. Thus it happened that from the angular and indirect nature of the entrance, it was impossible that any light, however brilliant, in the centre of the cavern, could be seen until the individual approaching it had come into a right line with it. This, however Patchy had not yet done. The first light visible was not the real one. On the contrary, it was ingeniously placed there for the purpose of throwing the shadow of the person advancing across the platform adjoining the innermost recess of the cavern, which was the occasional rendezvous of the Rapparees, when planning their operations in that part of the country. So strictly vigilant were these men at their meetings here, and indeed everywhere else, that a sentinel was always placed to watch the platform in question, and the moment a shadow was seen, a challenge was given to the intruder. Patchy had not made more than three or four steps when his person became distinctly visible, and in an instant a voice called out, in stern significant tones, that could not be misunderstood, " Who comes here ?" and a man immediately started forward with a loaded blunderbuss in his hand.

" A friend to the friends of my country," replied Patchy " Be aisy, will you ? It's Patchy that's in it."

" It's the voice of Patchy, but you must advance and show yourself ; we must read your face, Patchy, for fear there might be no more of Patchy than his tongue about you."

" Ah, Quee Harry, is it you ?" said Patchy, advancing and shaking hands with him ; then entering the inner cavern, he proceeded : " That's your plan, comrades ; keep a sharp lookout, and reason good you should ! You have the wealth of the country, the government, and the sogers, on watch for you ; so you see, as I said, you must have both your eyes and your ears about you. Well, and are you all safe ? None of you hanged yet, I hope !"

" Not one, Patchy, nor no danger of it ; we'll turn a corner on them at the long run."

" So you will, plaise God ; sure it's all for the good of the country that you're actin' as you're doin'. May the Lord reward you, and keep you from that worst and roughest of all blackguard weeds, by name—hemp. But where's the Captain ? I don't see *him* here. All's right wid *him*, I hope !"

" All's right, Patchy ; he is *out* to-night to meet a gentleman

on the new road tha. intends to *lend* him two or **three hundred**
pounds. He—the gentleman I mane—is to have three sogers
wid him for protection ; but that doesn't signify much,)ekase
the Captain has Shane Bearnah, James Butler, and strong
John M'Pherson,* all well armed, along wid him, and i. there
was three sogers more against them, it 'ud make little differ.
Here, Patchy, won't you have a *gauliogue* of the cratur to
warm your heart after your dark and ugly journey ?"

"I think I ought," said Patchy, " and, in truth, a dark and
ugly journey it is ; so here's wishin' us all long life and good
health, and that none of us may ever swallow lead or see his
own funeral. *Chiernah!* but that's the stuff, and it's bought
for three times less than nothin'."

The bottle was then sent about, but with great moderation ;
for drunkenness, when thrice repeated, was followed by ex-
pulsion from the gang. It is singular to reflect upon the
strange perversion and involution of moral feeling by which
this desperate and terrible confraternity was regulated. The
three great principles of their lawless existence were such as
would reflect honor upon the most refined associations. and
the most intellectual institutions of modern civilization. These
were : first, sobriety ; secondly, a resolution to avoid the
shedding of human blood ; and, thirdly, a solemn promise never
to insult or offer outrage to woman, but in every instance to
protect her. Yet, upon the basis of principles involving so
much that was noble and lofty in morality, was erected such
a superstructure of theft and robbery as Irelan l never saw,
either before the period we write of or since.

The present meeting was an annual one ; and such was the
alarmed state of the country, and so frequent were the attempts
made to disperse, or rather secure this celebrated and terrible
gang. but, above all, their leader, that they felt it would not

* There are real characters, and were part of his gang.

be safe to meet except on great or rare occasions, even in this remote and unknown cavern. At that period it was the last wild recess left them which had not been, one after another, discovered, and their anxiety to preserve the secret of its existence was great in proportion to the danger which its discovery would have brought upon them. There were present on this occasion none but the leaders of the wild and savage banditti that were then dispersed over all parts of the kingdom for to none else would the secret of their present place of meeting be communicated. Neither was the observance of the three principles we have alluded to made anything like a matter of conscience by a great number of the subordinate robbers, who frequently violated every one of them, or, in other words, committed murder, fell into drunken excesses, and threatened females with outrage and cruelty. The last, however, was certainly the rarest of their crimes.

Within the range of the wide district over which the sway of the great Rapparee of whom we write prevailed there was scarcely a single exception ever known—we believe only one— against the faithful adherence to the very letter as well as the spirit of these three fundamental regulations that he laid down for their conduct. This was owing, as we have every reason to believe, to the fact that their leader was a gentleman of a high and ancient Irish family, one of whose ancestors was knighted by Queen Elizabeth for important services rendered to her cause. And we may add here, that another of the descendants of his family, when George the Fourth visited this country, claimed his right of hereditary standard-bearer for Ireland, north of the Boyne, and had his claim admitted by my late friends Ulster King-at-Arms, Sir William Betham.

The appearance of the cavern in which they were assembled was very simple, and had nothing extraordinary about it except its large and ample space. Not a stalactite depended from the roof; but as a compensation for its want of natural ornaments, it was as dry as powder. If nature left it naked, however, art had supplied the deficiency. It was, in fact, not only a place of rendezvous, but a storehouse of arms, ammunition, and such a variety of diferent costumes as would puzzle and confound a modern pawnbroker. Every garb of the day was there, hanging from pegs driven into the sides of the cavern—from that of the tattered beggar to the rich and fashionable apparel of the wealthy gentleman, and from that of the common soldier to the exact uniform of his superior officers. The last were principally the property of their celebrated leader, who assumed them all on several occasions during the extraordinary and almost incredible variety of his exploits. Here also was their magazine, which consisted of a great variety of firearms, all carefully oiled and wrapped in flannel, so as to prevent them from becoming useless or dangerous by damp or rust, together with a considerable portion of gunpowder, preserved with equal care. Such large sums of money, too, and all the valuable plate which they had plundered from the gentry of the country, were deposited here for security, until the plate at least could be melted down and safely disposed of ; and for this purpose they had crucibles, and all the other necessary apparatus. The particular place, however, in which the treasure was deposited, being considered by their chief a temptation probably too strong for the honesty of some of them, was a secret known only to himself and Shane Bearnah, his confidant, and the next in command.

Having thus described the place of their annual and other extraordinary meetings, we will now recite the names and peculiar pursuits of those who were there assembled, for the purpose, as we have said, of debating upon the course of their proceedings during the next campaign; but it is to be remembered that their chief, together with three others : to wit,

Shane Bearnah, James Butler, and strong John M'P terson, were then absent, being engaged in the execution of a robbery. Neither is it to be forgotten that the names we are about to mention, as well as those we have given, are authentic and historical. The first in importance and in fame, at that period at least, although seldom mentioned now, was Captain Power, so called, not from any military title he had ever received, but in consequence of his position as the head and commander of the Munster robbers, or Rapparees. He was born at Kilvallen, in the county of Cork, and was the son of a gentleman who possessed a good freehold estate at that place. He had had a quarrel with his brother, after which he got into a lawsuit, which he lost. A writ of contempt of court having been issued against him, he spurned and defied its authority, and, as a matter of course, was outlawed. After some time he returned home,—and rather than be a burthen to his relations, took to the highway, and became the most celebrated robber that Munster ever produced. Like the great Rapparee who is the hero of this narrative, he never shed blood, and was remarkable for his kindness and charity to the poor. After he had been on the highway for some time, he was offered a pardon through the intercession of his friends ; but feeling an irresistible impulse for a life of adventure, he refused the mercy that was extended to him, and preferred the wild and excitable life of a bandit. He had come down from Munster to visit and see the great northern robber, from motives of curiosity and admiration. Their actual meeting, whilst each was ignorant of the person of the other, is so full of interest and romance, that we may probably give it on some future occasion. He remained with his northern brother for about twelve months, and is now present more as his friend than as one of his gang. First, then, on this occasion, we will mention him as—

Captain Power, a Gentleman Rapparee.

Paul Liddy, a Gentleman Rapparee.

William Peters, *alias* Delany.

Charles Dempsey, *alias* Cahir na Cappul, the renowned Horse-stealer, introduced into his novel of "the Boyne Water," by John Banim.

Manus M'O'Neil the Gold-finder, introduced into "Suil Duv," by Gerald Griffin,

Strong John McPherson,
Shane Bearnah, of whom above, } at present out with their leader.
James Butler,

John Mulhone,

James Carrick,

Quee Harry Donoghan, the Napper (stealer, prigger) of Ulster,

Patrick M'Tigh (M'Teague),

John Reilly,

Phil Galloge,

Pat Mill,

Arthur O'Neil, and

The famous O'Kelly, the Kilkenny man.

Now, most of these men have personal records left of their lives and deaths. They held high but subordinate appointments under their celebrated chief, and such of them as have not distinct biographies, are incidently mentioned by their clever and graphic biographer, Cosgrave, who was himself their contemporary, and if we are to be guided by a hint in what purports to be a letter to him—evidently written, however, by himself—there is reason to suppose that he was one of their own fraternity

CHAPTER V.

WHEN Patchy noticed Captain Power, who was then, as always, in the garb of a gentleman, he respectfully touched his hat to him, observing as he did it:

"I think I see a gentleman here who's a stranger to me—I'm Patchy Baccach, sir, the *setter*—and now that you know me, I hope you won't keep the advantage of me."

"Not at all, Patchy, I have heard of you from the chief; wa are a very valuable man, Patchy—I'm Captain Power."

"God bless my sowl, sir," replied Patchy, taking off his hat—"is it possible that the great Captain Power is one of us?"

"Yes, but only for a time, Patchy. I thought myself at the head of my profession, Patchy, and I came down here to have an interview with the Great Northern; but I soon found that clever and able as I considered myself, I had much to learn from him."

"Well, indeed, I'm not surprised at that, sir," replied Patchy, "for if ever there was a maricle at the business, he is one. He was never done but once, and that was by the Dundalk apprentice."

"How was that?" asked Power.

"Why, sir, there was a merchant in Dundalk who had a draft on another in Newry, for the sum of two hundred pounds. Such was his terror, howandever, of the Captain, that he was afeard either to go for the money himself, or to send for it by another. In this state of mind he was one day consultin' wid his wife as to what was best to be done in the matter, when his apprentice, a lad about sixteen, happened to overhear them. He offered to go for the cash, and said, he would let them cut the ears off his head if he did not bring it home safe to them Now, both the merchant and his wife knew he was a smart chap, and always had his wits about him ; so, after another consultation, they agreed to let him make the trial, and accordingly gave him the draft. Well, sir, the first thing he did was to saddle an ould entire horse, so lame wid the spavy that he could hardly go a mile an hour, an , what was worse than all, the brute, from sheer viciousness and a hell-fire temper, would suffer neither horse nor man to come near him on the road—the' prentice himself bein' the only person he would allow to handle or mount him. Well and good , the lad got two pounds changed into halfpence, which he tied in a bag—one half in each end, wid a string about the middle, and havin' mounted his horse, he went his way towards Newry ; when, as it happened, on comin' to a lonely part of the road, who comes up wid him but the Captain. The chap seemed very innocent, and soon tould him the whole story of the money ; and how he was to bring it back the next day. The Captain said it was wrong of him to mention the circumstance to any one, for 'fraid he might be robbed ; and on partin' gave him a guinea to drink his health and hire another horse if he wished.

"'When do you expect to be back, my lad,' he asked.

"'About this time to-morrow, sir,' replied the boy ; 'and by dad I wish I had you along wid me all the way, for then I'd have no fear of bein' robbed of it.'

"All right so far ; the lad got to Newry, where he remained all night ; and the next mornin', havin' got the cash in bank-notes, he sowed them up in the linin' of his waistcoat, and set out on his return home. Well, to make a long story short, he had just come to the same lonesome part of the road where he met the gentleman the day before, and, shure enough, there he met him again.

" Well, my good boy,' said the Captain, 'did you get the money ?'

"' Bedad I did so, sir,' replied the shaver, 'every penny.'

"' And hew did you get it ?' asked the gentleman.

"' Faix, in hard goold,' said the other ; ' and here I have it, a hundred in each end o' this bag ; but I wouldn't tell that, sir, to any one but yourself, for 'fraid I might be aised of it— but I know by your appearance you're a gentleman, and that I needn't be afeared of you.'

"' Yes, but hand me the money,' said the Captain, ' till I see if it's all right.'

"' I know it's right,' said the boy, ' for I counted it myself ; and, besides, my masther made me take an oath, before I left home, that afther I got it I wouldn't let it into any one's hands but my own.'

"' Hand it out immediately, said the Captain, 'I must have it.'

" But sir,' said the chap, 'my masther will blame me for it, and say that I made away wid it myself.'

"' Deliver the money immediately, you young scoundrel,' says the Captain, pulling out a pistol, ' or I'll blow your brains out.'

"' I couldn't think of doin' sich a thing,' says the youth ; ' I promised to let him cut my ears off if I didn't bring it safe to him, and I will, too.'

" The Captain immediately rode up to him, in ordher to secure it, but, lo and behould you, the devilish ould cappul (horse) the lad was on turns round and threw out at him and his horse, which made him keep his distance ; and, in the meantime, the cunnin' young vagabone moved him over to the roadside, and threw the bag that contained the coppers across the hedge, and a good distance into a quagmire that happened to be in the place.

"' If you want to get it, sir,' says he, ' you must go for it

bekasc I tuck an oath to my masther, that I wouldi t give it
into the hands of any one; and now he can't say I perjured
myself.'

"The Captain immediately lit down off his horse, hooked
him to the branch of a tree, and with a good deal of time and
strugglin' got through the hedge, and after that had quite as
much difficulty in wadin' through the quagmire. This ripe
youth, in the manetime, unhooked the Captain's fir.e horse—
mounted him, set off at full speed, laving him two pounds'
worth of coppers in a bag, and a spavined ould *garran*, as full
of venom and mischief as an egg is of mate, instead of the two
hundred pounds he expected; and what was betther still, rob-
bin' the robber of his fine horse before his own face into the
bargain. There, now, is the only case in which the Captain
was ever done; but, be my sowl, he was done there, and in
style, too."

"But did he ever recover his ·horse?" asked Captain
Power.

"The horse," replied Patchy, "was put to livery in Dundalk, and advertised; but I need not tell you that the Captain, *for a reason that he had,* never claimed him—but he
wrote a letter widout a name to his masther, statin' that his
owner made a present of him to the young rogue, in reward
for his cleverness and ingenuity. He never can tell that story
himself widout laughin' heartily, and wishin' that he had the
trainin' of the lad."

It is not to be supposed that these worthy Rapparees sat
here without the necessary requisites to keep them comfortable. There was a large fire, around which they disposed themselves on such temporary seats as they could procure, together
with an ample stock of provisions and other refreshments, such
as wine, whisky, brandy, and malt liquor, in abundance. Of
those they partook—some sparingly, some more freely—but

not one to excess or intoxication; for on this necessary point their Captain kept them in an excellent state of discipline

"Come, my bowld comrades," said Patchy, "let us have a glass of comfort, and amuse ourselves as well as we can un til the Captain and the others come back. Captain Power, here's long life, good health, and a happy death-bed to you; and, as I said before, may none of us ever see his own funeral! *Amin, a chiernah!*"

This was drank, and Patchy proceeded: " Come, Billy Peters, or Delany, or whatsomever you call yourself, let us hear a little of your skill and experience. You're nearly as great a horse-stealer as *Cahir na Cappul* there."

" Me !" replied Cahir, in his broken English—a man, by the way, in every lineament of whose face nature had set the stamp of thief and robber—"me, Patchy—fwhy now, Patchy, don't she knows dat I never staled a baste in my life. Sure I haven't gotten no causcience about stalin' 'em—I never staled any, sure."

"Well, if you don't stale them yourself, Cahir, you know who does, so that it all comes to the same thing. But you, Billy Peters, in the manetime, tell us something to amuse us and pass the time."

" Troth, the story I'm goin' to tell," replied Peters, "is as much *Cahir na Cappul's* there as mine; but sich as it is you shull have it."

" Ay, do," said Cahir, " tell her up for de gentlemin."

" Well, then," proceeded Peters, " some time after I got the bite from the girl that was whipped through the town of Maryborough, for several acts of thievin' she committed, and who palmed herself upon my father and me as Captain P——'s daughter, I became acquainted wid worthy *Cahir na Cappul* here; and, becoorse, I wasn't long a croneen of his until I tuck a strong fancy for horse-stealin'."

" You wor a big tief afore you comes to me," observed Cahir.

"Well, if I was, Cahir, you soon improved me. Troth, I was nothing till I knew you ; but no matter. Soon afther I got rid of my doxy, it so happened that I tuck a strong fancy to a fine sorrel horse, wid a bald face and a white foot, that belonged to a gentleman in the county of Carlow. I got into the stable one night, by means of a thing that I'm sure," he added, with a grin, "none of you ever heard of—a false key. It isn't, nor ever was, my custom to do a thing unfairly ; so, says I, whispering to the horse, 'have you any objection to come wid me and see the world ?' Throth, I thought it but fair and reasonable to put the question to him ; but, at any rate, devil a word he said against it. 'That's all right,' says I, 'silence gives consent ;' and off we went on the best of terms wid each other. Well, I sowld the horse at a good price, but the *toir* (pursuit) was soon up afther.me, and in a short time I was lodged in Carlow jail, wid every proof strong against me ; so that I saw clearly there was little else for me but to dance the pleasant jig called the 'Hangman's Hornpipe.' Not that I was much troubled about that either, in regard that I was once hanged before,* and escaped the noose twiist afterward, and all by raison of a charm I got against hangin' from the same woman that gave *Cahir na Cappul* there the enchantment that enables him, wid a weeshy whisper in his ear, to tame the wildest and wickedest horse that ever went upon four feet. Be this as it may, I was very much troubled about the matter, and hardly knew how to act. At last I bethought me of Cahir here, and sent to let him know how I was fixed. I desired him to look at the horse, and to find me out a mare as like him as possible, and to try and exchange the one for the other—otherwise I had little chance, as the evidence was

* A fact.

so clear against me.   Ah, troth, Cahir, my boy, it's you tha.
wasn't long gettin' me the mare I wanted, nor in giving in-
structions how to have the thing done.   The trial was now
within a day or two of comin' on, and the stolen horse was
put under the care of the jailor, as is usual, till it should
be over.   When Cahir's messenger arrived, he put up at a
place near the river-side, where the hostler used to water
the horse.   He had got acquainted wid him, and on this occasion asked him in to have a drink, to which he willingly con-
sented, lavin' the horse at the door.   In the manetime, the
animals were exchanged by a comrogue of the messenger's ;
and when the hostler came out, after gettin' his mornin', he
mounted the mare and rode her to the stable instead of the
horse.   Well, very soon afterward, in about an hour or so, my
trial came on, and, to tell the truth, every thing went against
me—nothing could be clearer than the evidence ; and the
judge was goin' to charge the jury, when I thought it was
time to speak :

" 'My lord,' says I, 'every man's life is precious to him.
You all think me guilty ; but I deny it, and will prove my
innocence, if you'll grant me one request.'

" 'What is it ?' asked the judge.

" 'It is, my lord,' says I, 'that the horse shall be produced
in coort.   When he is, if I don't show the whole world that
I'm wrongfully charged with the crime I'm in for, why, then,
hang me up as an example to all the horse-stealers in the kingdom ; and I'll go to my death willingly.'

" 'But how could the production of the horse save you ?
said the judge.

." 'My lord,' says I, 'I cannot tell you that till the horse
comes into coort.'

" 'My lord,' says my lawyer, 'as the poor man thinks his life
dependin' on it, surely his request ought to be complied with.'

" 'Very well,' said the judge, smilin', 'let the norse be pro
duced in coort.'

" 'The horse is my witaess, my lord,' says I, 'and will bring
ne out clear.'

" 'It is the first time I ever heard of such a witness,' said
the judge, laughin' outright, as did the whole coort ; 'but as
you think he'll serve you, it is but right that you should have
his testimony."

" 'We shall cross-examine him severely,' said the opposite counsel, 'and it'll go hard or we'll make him break
down.'

" By this time the whole coort was in roars of laughter, and
they were all on coals to see what would happen. Well, in a
short time the horse was brought into coort, and I turned
round to my prosecutor.

" 'Now, sir,' says I, 'do you swear positively and truly that
that is the animal you lost ?'

" 'I do,' says he ; 'by the virtue of my oath, that is my
horse—the very one you stole from me.'

" 'By the virtue of your oath, sir, whether is that animal a
horse or a mare ?'

" 'By the oath I've taken,' he says again, 'it's a horse, and
not a mare. It was a horse I lost, and that's the animal.'

" The short and the long of it was, that the animal proved
to be a mare, and not a horse at all. Such a scene was never
witnessed. Every one in the coort was in convulsions, with
the exception of my prosecutor, who had a face on him as long
as to-day and to-morrow. As for the jury, you'd tie them wid
three straws.

" 'Gentlemen,' said the judge, addressin' them as well as
he could speak tor laughin', 'you must acquit the prisoner.'

" 'We do, my lord,' said the foreman, 'we find a verdict of
acquittal.'

"'Let him be immediately discharged, then' said the judge. And so I was, comrades, and—here I am"

"Give Peter a glass for that," said Patchy "If that wasn't doin' them, I dunna what was."

"But, sure, as I tould you all, it was *Cahir na Cappul* here that desarves the credit of that; for what do you think he did? Why, he painted the mare so like the horse, that livin' eyes couldn't see the difference. Ah, Cahir! Cahir! what are we all in the horse-stalin' line, when compared wid you I'm middlin' myself, and Shane Bearnah's betther still, but neither of us could hould a candle to you at the business."

"I never staled a horse in my life," repeated Cahir; "sure every one knows dat I never stales no horses."

"Do you take apprentices still, Cahir?" asked Manns M'O'Neil, the gold-finder.

"Yes, I does," replied Cahir, "when I gets a good fwhee (fee) wid 'em. Many o' de Munster farmers does shend der shilders to me to larn the saicrits."

"And what fee do you charge, Cahir?"

"Why, frwhom whifty to a hundars pounds, and fwhor dat I finishes dem."

"Yes, Cahir," observed Power, drily, "I dare say you do."

This may seem strange, if not incredible, to our readers; but such was the fact. Some of the Munster farmers—men of wealth and substance, too—felt no scruple whatsoever in binding their sons to this celebrated cattle-stealer, in order that they might afterward pursue such theft as a trade. Cahir, however, by his multiplied process of ingenuity, almost elevated it to the rank of a science, although he himself did not know a letter in the alphabet.

That the singular fact of such apprenticeships argued a very loose notion of the rights of property, can scarcely be denied; but, on the other hand, it is not altogether without something in the shape of apology. The consciousness of wrong it is that constitutes guilt ; but here there was no such feeling.. The possession of property by Protestants was looked upon as an act of injustice by the Catholic population and the country at large. This property, they said, was oppressively wrested from their forefathers and themselves by arbitrary laws, and they consequently looked upon themselves as wholly possessing the justest and the strongest title to it. Under those circumstances, and with such impressions, we are not to feel surprised that the aboriginal Irish should consider them- selves morally justified in despoiling the possessors of it as far as they possibly could with safety to themselves. This feeling was peculiarly strong in Munster, where the Rapparees and Tories actually succeeded, by their outrages upon both person and property, in frustrating every attempt to settle that country with a Protestant population.

"Come, Manus, you innocent babe of a goold-finder," said Patchy, "have you none of your exploits to tell us? Take a glass, man, and let the great Captain Power hear what you can do."

"Och !" replied Manus, with a shrug that indicated great simplicity, and in broken English, too, "sure it's a simple boy I am, and knows nuthin' about roguery—sarra tiug, now. I was borned honest, so I was, and de midwife said, when she seed my innocent face—' af I has a sowl in my bodies,' says she, 'dat child will come to great wealt' yet, and 'ill have much *arraghids* (money), and will make many peoples big wit mo- nies and skileens o' goold and riches—dat innocent child will— ay, indeed, now."

"Well, but, Manus," said Patchy, "we all know that you're an innocent boy, and has lashins of goold and jewels at your disposal; and that it's fear of the lord o' the manor that makes you sell them in private, poor *gorson*. But in the manetime,.

what if you'd give us the story of the ingot that you sould to the banker in Dublin."

Manus gave another shrug, indicative of his usual simplicity, and put an oafish grin upon his naturally blank features, that gave him literally the expression of a born idot.

" Is it dat I'm to tonl yez, den ?" said he.

"Ay," replied Patchy, "just that same. *Chiernah !*" he added, "look at him ! Wouldn't any one think that he didn't know Saturday from Sunday ? Go on, Manus ; Captain Power wants to hear it."

'Well den—yez must know that I had an ingit of raal gould, that was in woit twelve onnces to de ounoels, nayder more nor lesh ; and bein' in Dublin upon an experition to rise monies upon her, bekase de landlord was goin' to put my cattles in de pound—do you see—to sell' em aff for de rint—bad luck to awl rints and landlords, any way. I wint in de dresh of a middlin' farmer, wid my ingit rowled up in paper, and I fonnd him shettin' in a nice room by himshefs.

·"' Well, my man,' says he, ' whats do ye want wid me ?'

"' Fwhy, your honor,' shiz I, "it's well known dat you undercomstand all de onts and ins about monies, an' I come to you out o' no preference or respect at awl, but bekase it's misreported be awl parties dat you're a shentleman.' So he laughed.

"' But what is your bizness wid me, my good man ?' shis he.

"' Why, de landlord, your honor, and bad luck to him !'

"' But what have I to do wid your landlord ?' he shed.

"' Ah ! your worship,' shiz I, ' he's gooin' to *drive* me, af I don't have de rint for him be next Monda.'

·"' And how can I help you, my poor man ?' shiz he. ' What do you want wid me ?'

"' I wants to rise some monies on dis, shir,' shiz I, takin' de ingit out o' de paper she was rowled in. ' She's raal goold,

shir, and has been in our fwhamily for three or fwhor genera-
tions—but I'm not goin' to sell her, shir—but to rise monies
on her, bekase, shir, dere's an owld prowhccy in de family, dat
if we part wid her for gud, we'll never have luck or grace,
ayder here or thereafter.'

"'You wish to lave her in pledge, den?' shiz he.

"'Dat's de very ting, yer honor,' shiz I.

"'Well, den,' shiz he, 'you must wait awhile, till I shend it
to my gooldsmit, to try whether she's raal goold or not.'

"So he shent it off wid a messenger, and in a short time he
come back wit a uote fwhrom de gooldsmit, sayin' dat she was
raal goold.

"'Now, how much do want to rise an her?' shiz he.

"Well, to tell de troot, I axed more nor I knew he would
give. He wanted to buy her, but as I shed befwhore, I twold
him I only wanted to rise monies enough on her to pay de
rint, and save my brave cattles, so he made me an offer, but I
refused to take it, and takin' up my ingit, I rowled her agais
in de papers, and left him. After I had gone frhom him,
mavrone, oh, but I begnn to repint, so takin' out de brass
ingit, dat was gilt, and as like de oder as two pays, I went
back.

"'Plaise your honor,' shiz I, 'I have shanged my mind—
I'll take your offer; but take care of her fwhor me, bekase
if I lost her, de family 'ud never prospher, nayder here nor
thereafter.'

"Wid dat he paid me de monies, and put de ingit into a
press widout wanst lookin' at her, and I come away wid my
raal ingit snug in my pocket. It was on dat day de flags of
Dublin got so hot for my poor feet dat I couldn't remain any
time in dat beautiful city, for fears o' burnin' my soles; so I
left it, and wint to Connaught, fere de devil a much I got,
bekase it's a poor hole, and de peoples didn't understand En-

gfish, aldough I wished to pass fwhor a gentleman of book-larnin', dat understood nuttin' br: de English langridge, and several tings o' dat kind."

Many other anecdotes, detailing either the ingenuity or daring character of their exploits, were narrated, and when Manus had concluded his, Patchy, who acted also as their cup-bearer and butler, resolved to reward him with a glass.

" Come, my poor innocent lad," said he, handing him a bumper, " wet your whistle wid this—*it's* no counterfeit, any way, but the raal stuff—and here, you sentry, that's on the look-out there, watchin' for shadows, come and taste something that has substance in it. I don't think the sogers will run away wid us to-night, at any rate."

Manus took off his glass ; and the man who discharged the duty of sentinel joined them, as he had been invited, but had scarcely finished his, when a man in the uniform of a British officer sprang forward, exclaiming :

"Villains ! surrender this moment, and offer no resistance. You are my prisoners. I arrest you in the king's name !"

Every man present sprang to his feet, and secured his arms, and in a moment there were at least a dozen loaded pieces presented at him.

" Stop—hold, my friends !" exclaimed Power, seconding his words with a commanding motion of his hand; " keep quiet, and be cool ; injure him not at present, until we shall see the upshot of this. You know it is against our principles to shed blood unnecessarily, and only in self-defense. Let me speak to the gentleman—you know he is only discharging his duty ; but we, also, have a duty to discharge, and we shall discharge it. Now, sir," he added, addressing the officer, "what is your business here ?"

"To arrest and secure every man of you," replied the officer : resistance on your part is worse than useless. I have your retreat here surrounded by a company of soldiers; so that your escape is impossible."

"So is yours," replied Power. "You are an Englishman, I perceive, by your accent?"

"I am—I do not deny it."

"Well, then, you are our prisoner and our hostage; surround and disarm him."

The officer, who, by the way, had a pistol in each hand, stepped back.

"Forbear," said he; "I shall take at least two lives before I surrender, and mine, I know, you may take also. I know, too, that you may overpower me, and slay me where I stand, but that will not secure yourselves; for among my men it will only add a spirit of vengeance to a sense of duty. Now, mark me, I have a proposal to make; it argues neither courage nor gallantry on your part to surround and overpower by numbers a single man, as I am. Hearken now, if you be brave men, as they say you are. If there be any one individual among you who thinks himself stout enough to take me prisoner, and succeeds in doing so, I will submit without taking life; but if there be not, and that you attempt to overpower me by numbers, as I said, then most assuredly will I take two lives from among you, perhaps more, for my sword is sharp and trusty, and has never failed me yet."

"Be it so," replied Power; "it is a fair and manly challenge, and I myself accept it with pleasure."

"Pardon me, my friend!" exclaimed Paul Liddy, another gentleman Rapparee, and, except M'Pherson, considered the strongest and most active man in Ireland, as well as the most determined—"pardon me, my friend. In anything where courage is necessary, no man could take place before you; you are stout, too, I grant, as well as brave; but I don't think that, with all your strength, and all your bravery to boot, and I do not undervalue either the one or the other, you'd have any chance with that powerful officer. No, my friend, that task naturally falls to me, and I must have it."

"I should prefer you," observed the officer; "for you appear to me to be one of the strongest and finest looking men I ever saw."

"Very well, then," replied Liddy; "if I secure you single-handed, you are our prisoner and hostage."

"And if I secure you?" added the officer.

"Such a supposition is out of the question," replied Liddy; "but if you do, we will allow you to depart in safety, upon the condition that you pledge your honor, as an officer and a gentleman, that you will withdraw your men: for upon no other condition will you ever leave this place, or, at least, be set at large from among us."

"That is to say, whether I win or lose, your decision is to go against me," replied the officer. "That is not fair; which of you is the Captain? I should prefer dealing with him."

"Our Captain is not here at present," replied Liddy; "if he were, to no other hand would be assigned the task which I am about to undertake—a task which to him would be an easy one."

"Well," said the other, stepping back into the clear ground, "come on; after this matter shall be decided we will talk upon the subject of withdrawing my men."

He then put his pistols in his breast pockets, placed himself in readiness, and desired the gigantic Liddy to advance.

The contest was not a pugilistic one, but simply a trial as to which of them could seize, put down, and overmaster the other, so as to make him admit his defeat, and yield himself a prisoner. The struggle was, indeed, a terrible one in point of muscular exertion, activity, skill, and power; and so tremendous and equally balanced were the strains and efforts on

both sides, that the hopes and fears of the spectators rose and
fell as the one or other individual prevailed   At length, after
a contest of fifteen minutes, one of Liddy's legs was forced into
a position which put him somewhat off his centre, and quick
as lightning his opponent availed himself of the circumstance,
and shot him with great violence to the earth, which was nearly
as hard as stone.   He lay stunned for a time, and the other,
placing his foot upon his body, pointed to him, and said :

"Pray, who is the prisoner now ?"

"You are," said three or four voices behind him, and he
found himself fast pinioned.

"We will not injure you, sir," said Power ;   "but we shall
tie you neck and heels until we get free from this cavern.   We
are outlaws, sir, and you cannot expect us to observe the force
of any law or principle at variance with our own safety.   As
for the trial of strength and activity which has just taken
place, let it pass as an idle thing.   You are evidently a brave
man, and a stout one ; but we must consider for our safety
and our lives.   Get the cords forward, and bind him fast."

"Ha !" exclaimed the officer, in his own voice, who at once
changed the whole coutour of his face into its natural expression.   "Well done, my dear Power ; any other conduct
would have been wrong—safety before everything.   There
now, let me go ; but you see that if I *had* been a British
officer, and acquainted with the place of your retreat, I could
have taken every man of you."

It is unnecessary to describe their amazement on discovering
that it was their own Captain who had thus imposed upon
them.

"Good heavens !" exclaimed Power, " are you nothing more
than a mortal man ?"

"Nothing more," replied the other ; " and, I think, you
will admit a very good one, too—as he must be who could

prove an overmatch for the brave and powerful Paul Liddy
Raise him up, poor fellow. I hope he is not seriously hurt."

Paul, however, soon recovered, and after shaking himself
and feeling his bones, declared that, with the exception of a
ringing in his ears, he felt conscious of no other injury.

"Now," said their chief, "how did it happen that I was
able to surprise you as I did? for that is a serious question."

Patchy now advanced, and, with rather a rueful face, took
the whole blame upon himself, and gave a candid account of
the affair, exactly as it happened.

"I asked Pat Mill, who was on guard," said he, "to come
over and have a glass, and while he was takin' it, you boulted
in upon us. *Chiernah*, but you're the wonderful man ; for I
believe in my sowl you could change yourself into anything."

"Well," replied the other, "let that be a warning to you
all ; never on any possible occasion, or by the force of any
temptation whatsoever, to neglect your appointed duties. I
shall overlook this breach, but not another. Get me some
food."

The three individuals who had been out with him now entered ; but not without being duly challenged. They and their
commander then sat down, and did ample justice to the sub-
stantial fare that was placed before them. When the meal
was finished the Captain desired them to open a bottle of wine,
of which he, Power, and Liddy partook.

"Well, Liddy," said he, "I was anxious to have a trial of
strength with you, and I've had it. You are a stronger man
than I am, but you have neither my activity, skill, nor energy ;
but, in the meantime, you need not feel abashed by being put
down by me. Indeed, it was chance favored me, or it might
have been otherwise."

"Did you succeed to night!" asked Power.

"Certainly. They prepared for resistance ; but I shouted

out, as if I had a reinforcement at hand—' Fire yo1, there, from the shrubbery, if they attempt to resist !' But they did not, and here are two hundred pounds safe. I care not about it, however. I am grieved and vexed, for I heard a tale to-night that has filled me with sorrow."

"What !" said Liddy, "none of our other men taken, or our retreat discovered ?"

"No," replied the Captain ; "but a most diabolical outrage has been perpetrated upon one of my best friends—upon the daughter of a man who stood by me in the day of my distress with good faith and honor—I mean Brian Callan, whose daughter has been forcibly taken away by that unprincipled profligate, Cornet Lucas."

" Ay," said Quee Harry, " that's the scoundrel who swears he will never rest till he secures you, and sends your head to Armagh jail."

" 'I met young M'Mahon to-night," proceeded the other, " and he told me the whole story. The poor fellow is in a state of distraction, and swears that if he finds out Lucas to be the author of the outrage he will shoot him stone dead. I told him he was mistaken, and that Lucas was innocent of it."

" And why, sir," said Patchy, "did you do so ? Lucas is the man, and it happens that I can tell you all about it. He's after that good and beautiful girl for months, and she wasn't far from stabbin' him to the heart in her father's house one day not long ago. I was at the back windy, and seen it wid mine own eyes. Why, then, did you tell him it wasn't Lucas that done it ?"

" I had two reasons, Patchy ; the first was, that if M'Mahon was to shoot him he would be hanged ; and the second, that I wish to have the punishment of the worthy Cornet as my own work. Neither will I take the scoundrel's life. You all k ,ow I am against shedding blood from both feeling and principle, unless in defense of my own life, which is an act of self-preservation, natural not only to man, but to every animal that breathes. I shall give him a worse punishment, notwithstanding. Now, that girl's father, Brian Callan, has paid me his tribute for years, and specially during my cripplehood, when he generously increased it. For this I was and am solemnly bound to preserve all his movable property *within doors and without;* and if it happens to be taken away I am either to restore it or pay him the value of it. It is true that the children of a family do not come under this stipulation ; but that matters not. So help me, Heaven, if he were an utter stranger to me, no matter what his creed or religion, I would leave no stone unturned to restore his child and punish the villain who took her away."

" But how can you restore her, sir, if you don't know where she is ?" asked Patchy.

"Believe me, Patchy, I shall soon find out. When I had my protection from government for three years, through the influence of Cornet Montgomery and his friends, I became acquainted with an intimate friend of this Lucas."

"Take your time, sir," said Patchy, interrupting him ; "I can tell you where she is, and that is, strange as you may think it, in the very heart of Armagh barracks."

" Ay, and from the very heart of Armagh barracks I shall take her, Patchy—rest assured of that ; but, in the meantime, tell me all you know about the transaction ?"

Patchy then gave him a full and perfect account of the circumstances, together with the number of the window, reckoning from the corner of the range, not omitting the fact that he would find three round stones, each of about two pounds weight, lying together exactly under it. He then showed him Cornet Lucas's protection, which the other said he would keep for a time, but only for a short time, as he said it might be useful to him in consequence of the peculiar situation in which he stood.

"But now, Patchy," said he, "mark me, don't breathe a syllable to any one of her friends concerning the place of her concealment, not even to her father's family, or her lover, M'Mahon ; keep it a profound secret, otherwise you will obstruct and utterly destroy the plan I have conceived, not only for her liberation, but for Lucas's shame and punishment."

Patchy, who was well aware of the force and energy of will which characterized the Rapparee, as well as of his wonderful fertility in expedients, promised that he would faithfully observe the injunction laid upon him, although he understood not its purport. Other business of importance to themselves and their designs was then gone into, and all their arrangements and appointments made for the next six months.

CHAPTER VI.

THE individual who commanded this formidable gang of Rapparees was, considering his position in the world, probably the most extraordinary man of his age, or of any age before or since. Carte, in his life of Ormond, after giving an authentic account of his death, states, that for a series of many years he kept the whole province of Ulster, with a considerable portion of Leinster, in such a state of terror and alarm as was almost incredible. He asserts, that the whole military force of the kingdom was not able to apprehend him, nor to preserve the peace of the country, or establish the security of life and property so long as he lived. It is true he was often made prisoner, but he never failed, by the exercise of his wit, ingenuity, or courage, to escape from the hands of his captors. His personal and mental accomplishments were amazing. That, however, is not extraordinary; for, as we said, the man was not only a gentleman by birth, but Count of the French Empire—a title which was conferred upon him during his residence in that country. He is said to have been the most perfect specimen of a man in the kingdom. He was well educated, and could speak the English, Irish, and French languages to perfection. His athletic powers, strength, and activity, were unrivaled, but if there was anything more extraordinary about him than another, it was his wonderful Protean power of assuming all characters with such ease and effect, that when he chose to discard his own, and assume another, his most intimate friend could not recognize him. He could pass himself, whenever he wished, for an Englishman, Scotchman, or Frenchman, without the slightest risk of detection, and such was the flexibility of the muscles of his face, that he could transform himself into an old man of seventy with scarcely an effort.   He is said to have been the handsomest man of his day, and of the most perfect symmetry.   We may judge of what his popularity among the people must have been, when, notwithstanding the enormous rewards that were offered by the government of the day for his head, living or dead, he was never betrayed during a period of about twenty-five years, either by any of the people or his own gang.   The sum of five hundred pounds had been offered for his apprehension— equal to a thousand of our money—but without effect.   This, in a great measure, was owing to his generosity to the poor and struggling people, whom he frequently assisted, and to his liberality in sharing his plunder with his own men.

Having left their place of rendezvous, his intention was to lose no time in rescuing Rose Callan from the clutches of Lucas, for which he had formed a plan that was at least a feasible. if not a complete one.   In order to accomplish this with proper effect and success, he repaired to a village near Four-Mile House, between Dundalk and Newry, where he was resolved to make the necessary preparations for the liberation of poor Rose from her frightful captivity.   Having letters to write. and other matters to arrange, he selected the cottage of a friendly family for the purpose.   Here, however, he had not remained long, when a young girl came in, with looks full of terror, and exclaimed :—

"Oh, sir, run for your life ; an officer and a whole lot o sogers is comin' to the house !"

It was at the time scarcely daybreak, and the sun had not risen, so that it was difficult to see a person at any considerable distance.   He immediately fled, and when the Captain and twenty men from Caradevlin temporary barracks arrived at the house, they found that the bird had flown.   In order for their better success in his pursuit and capture, they had, before leaving barracks, stripped themselves to their waistcoats, and brought nothing with them but their muskets and bayonets, and some provisions in their pockets. Having expressed much indignation at his escape, they were about to retrace their way, when they heard him call out from an adjacent hill, bidding them defiance. This was an egregious piece of folly on his part, but frequent success had made him daring, and he has been known to bring risk and danger on his own head, by his extraordinary love for adventure, and a reckless confidence in his own powers. The officer in command immediately dispersed his party into three divisions, and resolved to give him instant pursuit. He himself, with ten men, were to maintain the chase in the direct centre, whilst five men on each side were to form the wings at a distance of a quarter of a mile.

In this manner the pursuit was maintained until noon, without allowing him a moment's rest. Several of the men, however, became exhausted and unable to continue the chase at so severe a pace. Only four were able to keep him in view—which they did notwithstanding the roughness of the country and the difficulties they had to surmount in ascending the hills, to which he took, knowing that his chances in the open and inhabited country would have been much against him. When evening came on he concealed himself in a clump of furze, on the side of of a hill, which was covered with them, hoping to escape during the night to a small village about half a mile distant, where he knew he had friends. In this design he was sadly disappointed. His pursuers, although he had outrun them half a mile, suspecting that he had concealed himself, discharged a gun as a signal to their lagging companions, and in the meantime resolved to watch the place until they should arrive. When the whole body was assembled they instituted a diligent search, but, fortunately for him, without success. They then held another council, not many yards from the place of his con-

cealment, when they came to the resolution of resting and
refreshing themselves with the slight provisions which they had
brought with them—for it was clear they had not calculated
upon so long and difficult a pursuit. The Rapparee overheard
their conversation, and had made up his mind to attempt
escaping ; but from this he was prevented by the brightness
of the night, and the fact that the soldiers felt it necessary to
keep themselves warm by walking about the very spot where
he lay. It was in a slight hollow, or small excavation in the
ground, over which the furze met, but not apparently to such
a depth as would afford cover or shelter to any person. The
men now began to feel the pangs of hunger severely ; and as
daybreak arrived, observing a smoke at a distance, they repaired to it in the hope of procuring refreshment. Instead of
finding only one house, however, they found a village, where
they procured fresh provisions, of which they stood very much
in need. Having satisfied themselves, they were returning to
renew the chase, when they observed a man at some distance,
running towards a cabin that stood on the side of the hill.
The Rapparee, however, on looking behind him, and perceiving
his pursuers, at once altered his course, and the pursuit was
renewed with fresh vigor. The chances now were all to
nothing against him, the soldiers having recruited their
strength by the refreshments they had taken, whilst he naturally felt the twofold exhaustion of fatigue and hunger. On
that night, having still baffled and escaped them, he sheltered
himself as well as he could on the side of a mountain, where
he remained nearly famished, until daybreak, when, weak and
jaded, he repaired to the house of a fr'end in order to get
something to eat. His pursuers, in the meantime, had only
lost sight of him, but had no intention, by any means to give
him up. As the Rapparee approached the house, he was
attacked by a dog, who kept up a loud and incessant barking

at him before he entered the dwelling. His pursuers, who, although out of sight, were within hearing of the dog, immediately came up in a body and surrounded the house just as the object of their pursuit had sat down, with a cake of bread, some butter, and a jug of new milk before him. It was now the beginning of the third day since he had tasted food, and being almost spent and broken down, he was about to recruit his strength with the provisions that were before him, when the officer of the party made his appearance, and with much courtesy, which the Rapparee returned with the air of a perfect gentleman, said :

"Sir, you will excuse me if I say that I cannot feel at all sorry for having at last overtaken you—no easy task I assure you. A pursuit of more than two days is rather a trying affair to all of us ; but it so happens that we have you after a long run for it. Of course, you are aware that I have the king's warrant for your apprehension, and that you are now my prisoner."

"Sir," replied the Rapparee, "I acknowledge both. I am certainly your prisoner, and shall comply with your orders immediately. Recollect, however, that you have been in pursuit of me these two days past, with a speed and vigor which reflect the highest honor upon your spirits and physical powers, and that during all that time I have not tasted a single morsel of food. I am, indeed, incapable of proceeding just now without refreshment, unless you should come to the resolution of carrying me. I appeal then, sir, both to your courtesy as a gentleman, and your humanity as a man, to permit me to breakfast before I accompany you. When I shall have finished you may conduct me wherever you wish ; and, I assure you, it is no small honor to have secured the great Rapparee of the North."

"God forbid," replied the Captain, "that I should discharge

my duty in either an ungentlemanly or inhuman spirit The request you ask is not only reasonable but necessary, and shal' be granted."

The officer withdrew from the room, but stationed himself with eight men at the door, whilst twelve others surrounded the house, rendering escape apparently hopeless. When the Rapparee had finished his meal he paused for a brief space, and at once seizing his blunderbuss, he approached the door, and covering the officer with it, said :

" Now, sir, you have taken me prisoner, and I admit it. I demand *house-room* and *car-room*, which, if you refuse I shall discharge my blunderbuss into your body, and you shall die with me. I expect nothing but death, and I shall not die unavenged. I have but one life to lose ; you can take no more ; but, perhaps, I shall make three or four of you bear me company."

The audacious spirit of this language surprised the commander of the party, who felt himself so completely taken aback that he could not for some moments return an answer. During this apparent hesitation the Rapparee bounded off, and as the men felt also astounded, and stood, besides, in each others' way, so that they could not for a couple of minutes fire at him ; it so happened that he gained a space of about fifty yards' distance from them before he heard the cracking of their carabines after him. This, together with the time lost in reloading their pieces, gave him such an advance in the pursuit, invigorated as he felt himself, too, by a good breakfast, that he shot far ahead of them, got out of sight, and ultimately made a clear escape, to the shame and mortification of the crestfallen but gentlemanly officer and his party.

In the meantime, we must return to the pitiable Rose Callan, who is still secreted in the place chosen for her dreary and terrible captivity. Lucas's diabolical project of starving her into compliance was, from the moment of his last (and first) visit to her, deliberately acted on. During the first twenty-four hours the distraction and agony of mind incidental to the fearful situation in which she found herself prevented her from bestowing scarcely a thought upon food or nourishment. Her reflections turned altogether upon her imprisonment, and the brutal purpose for which it had been brought about. The pressure of the anguish she experienced was sometimes so severe that she fell into paroxysms of distraction that made her fear for her senses. These again were succeeded by dull and heavy periods of gloom, during which she felt her mind stupefied and collapsed to such a degree that she could scarcely think at all. Her reason became chaotic and pressed down by a lethargic stupor, which alarmed her far more than the acute attacks of distraction which she suffered. At the close of the second day, however, she felt herself assailed by a new and formidable adversary, to wit, want of food. This attack was keen, close, and personal. Her other sensations had to do with her mind and feelings ; but this dealt doubly with her physical system and its natural demands. Henceforth commenced a struggle between her apprehensions of insult and ruin, and the cravings of her appetite for sustenance, which may possibly be conceived, but cannot be described in language The refinement of the plan adopted for subjugating her will and consequently of overcoming her virtue, was, in its cruel, unmanly, and cowardly spirit, worthy of the devil himself. Here the innocent girl was placed, with two of the most terrific antagonists to contend with—a dread of becoming the victim of this ruffian, and the bootless struggle against the wasting pangs of famine, which were now beginning to consume her. When her mind passed from the contemplation of the one to that of the other, she felt the alternations of the prospect such as made her wish a thousand times that she were

dead.   On the beginning of the third day she felt such a sen
sation in the region of her stomach, as for a time, at least,
banished all other considerations.   The deadly spirit of famine
had got in there, and its demands were not only clamorous and
importunate, but painful and agonizing to the last degree.
Perhaps she would not have felt it thus keenly, had not her
imagination been so dreadfully excited by the apprehension of
ruin, which she knew it was designed to bring upon her.   Be
this as it may, the sufferings which she experienced, as resulting from it, when taken into consideration with the horrible
object connected with its infliction, nearly drove her mad.
Once every day the hag of perdition came to see her, with a
view of ascertaining whether the murderous process was likely
to succeed ; but poor Rose, during the first two days, treated
her like an incarnate demon—as she was—produced her skean,
and commanded her out of the room, asservating that she
would prefer death a thousand times sooner than the dishonor
that was proposed to her.   During the wretch's visit at the
close of the second day, she pointed to the decanter of port
wine which she had left behind, and assuming a look of something like compassion, said :

"Poor girl ! afther all, I pity you ; and bad as you think
me, you see I wouldn't take away that wine, for 'fraid that
truth might come upon you.   At any rate, take a glass of it
from time to time, and you'll find that it will compose your
mind, and do you good."

Rose felt even that a kindness ; but up to this period she
had experienced no thirst.   The satanic suggestion, however,
soon did its work.   It was hunger that had pressed upon her
heretofore, and it was not likely that she would ever have
thought of thirst, were it not for the vile woman's mention of
it.   Henceforth the sense of it, whether imaginary or real,
was associated with the wolfish pangs of famine, which deso

ated her within. Poor girl! Now were those two harpies
devouring her, sometimes alternately, according as the raven-
ous spirit of the one or otl er predominated, and sometimes
both together, wringing her failing heart with a double agony

On the beginning of the fourth day her strength was nearly
gone ; and it is to be remembered, that during all that time
she had had no sleep. For the first two days, apprehension of
violence kept her awake; but after hunger had set in, sleep
was physically impossible. It is known that those who labor
under a long period of famine never sleep, or if they enjoy
anything like a wakeful slumber, the agony of what they
suffer never ceases, but is felt in all its poignancy, probably
with more acuteness. Whether asleep or awake, in this
state, she dreamt she was at home, and eating voraciously
at her father's table, but could never feel satisfied. Sometimes she thought she drank, too ; but that her thirst was only
increased by what she drank. These tantalizing hallucinations,
however, were as bad, if not worse, in point of suffering, than
the awaking reality. Her prayers to God during this dreadful and inhuman trial, though distracted, were incessant. She
now began to feel as if all corporal weight or gravity had left
her ; her limbs were as light as feathers, she thought, but so
feeble, that when she sat, and wished to rise again, she could
not do so without several efforts. She pulled the skean out of
her bosom, and felt, to her consternation, that if it were necessary for her defense, she was unable to use it.

In the meantime, visions of home, of her parents, of her beloved brothers, and of her lover, were perpetually flitting before
her, and mingling themselves with the dreadful and manifold
sufferings which were distracting and pressing her down to
death. She saw the skies red with fire, and angels and de-
mons approaching her from the tumultuous firmament ; reason,
in fact, was tottering on its throne, and the course of thought

so completely broken and disturbed, that she was little short
of a maniac. There was a looking-glass in the room, and she
staggered over to it, not with any intention of looking into it,
but a mere accident resulting from her feebleness. She caught
a glance of herself, however, and stood for a moment to con-
template her own image. But, alas, what a picture was there
for her to look upon! The change which so short a period
had made in her was awful—frightful. Her flesh was gone
almost to emaciation; her eyes, once so brown and sparkling,
were lit up by the dull, deadly glare of famine; her cheek
bones stood out; her nose seemed crimpled and drawn in;
and the skin of her face appeared tightened and shining, as is
the case with those who are about to pass out of life after a
long and wasting illness. At this moment the tortures of
hunger and thirst beset her with such an unrelenting fury, that,
as she knew she had nothing to eat, she resolved to swallow
a portion of what was in the decanter. With this purpose
she tottered over toward the chimney-piece on which it stood,
and endeavored to take it down. Whether she was unable
to do this, or whether the Providence of God came to her aid,
we shall not presume to determine, but the fact is, that the
decanter fell out of her hands, and was smashed to pieces on
the iron fender, its contents, of course, being spilled about.
She would have wept at this, but she had no tears to shed;
the dry agony which shriveled her up had absorbed them
all.

When the decanter was broken, and its contents scattered
about the fireplace, some strong and heavy smell proceeded
from it, which nearly sickened her. Still the hunger and the
thirst were at her vitals, but principally the former, and if she
attempted to turn from the torture they inflicted, she was met
by the under-current of terror which resulted from the contemplation of the fate that was before her, and the con-

sickness of her incapacity to defend herself. She then reached with some difficulty an arm-chair, into which she rather fell than sat, and having covered her face with her hands, she groaned aloud as well as her enfeebled strength would allow her. In a few minutes after this the hag came into the room, and having looked upon her with something like alarm, she approached her, and putting one of her hands into the poor girl's bosom, drew out the skeau which she had kept, and looked upon as the best means for her protection. Alas ! the faint but earnest struggle she made was pitiful, and ought to have extorted compassion from a fiend.

"Oh, don't take it from me," she whispered, in a low, tremulous, but pleading voice. "As you hope for mercy before the throne of judgment, don't—don't leave me altogether defenseless ! Oh, think that I am a woman asking mercy from a woman. Do not—oh, do not." And as she spoke she strove to retain the grasp of it as well as she could; but her fingers were too feeble to hold it, and as for her general strength, it was quite gone. She then entreated her for a little food, in such tones of supplication as none but some human devil, devoted body and soul to the service of Satan—as she was— could have resisted.

"Oh !" she exclaimed, "for the love of God, do not let me die of hunger. A little food—but a mouthful or two of anything that will keep life in me. Do you forget that there is a God above you, who looks on at your cruelty, and will punish it ? Have you no heart, no feelings for one of your own kind? You are murdering me; but if you wish to do it, take this skean and plunge it into my heart, and then I will be out of pain, and beyond the reach of villainy : by taking my life you will save me; but if you cannot be kind enough to do so, then, for the sake of mercy—for the sake of God—bring me a little food, even but a little, for I am surely dying. I did not ask it from you before, because I had no thought that I was so near death as I find I am."

The old woman immediately secured the dagger, but said not a word ; indeed, she had not spoken at all since she came into the room, but took her departure, locking the door, as usual, after her. When she was gone the poor girl pressed her temples with her hands ; but after a little time a peculiar change came over her. She wrung her hands, and burst into a fit of laughter. She felt herself without hope—beyond this she could neither think nor reason now—and in a few minutes her prison-room rang with the maniac laughter of her despair.

In this state we shall leave her, until we look after some others of our *dramatis personæ*.

When the old woman left her, the wretch hobbled with more than usual haste to Lucas's room, whom she found writing a letter.

" Here, sir," said she, " Here is her dagger, at any rate ; but then I am afeared——"

" What are you afraid of now, Pugshy ?" *

" Troth, sir, I'm afraid she's dyin', and that we've carried the thing too far. The decanter, too, is broken, and the wine spilt, so that *that* chance is lost."

Just at this moment an orderly soldier came in, and handed the worthy Cornet a letter, on the back of which was written the words, " *Haste and attention !*" He immediately opened it, and read as follows :

" MY DEAR LUCAS : Do you wish to have your name made famous for ever, and to become a Colonel in twelve months; aye, and to secure five hundred pounds besides ? If so, get a dozen men, and proceed without a moment's delay to the Four-Mile House, where the great Rapparee is lying wounded,

* A vulgar and derisive name for Peggy.

after having escaped from and played the devil with Captain Nisbet, who, by the way, is going to be cashiered for letting him slip through his fingers. Lose not a moment, you profligate ! If you happen to be in pursuit of a pretty girl, give it up for the present, at least until to-morrow, and do what the Irish government, with all the military force in the kingdom, could not do—that is, to secure the person of this modern Proteus. I will call at your rooms in the course of the day ; so leave your keys with the old woman, for I shall exercise a sharp appetite, and allay a violent thirst upon whatever I can find in your larder. You are now on the way to fame and promotion, if you act with spirit ; and I shall soon be on my way to the barracks, for the sole purpose of seeing you fetch this devil of a man home with you as a prize that will make your fortune. That my moustache and whiskers may flourish, but I am delighted at the chance thus offered to you. Seize upon it, my boy, and you are a made man.

      "Ever thine,   GEORGE GRAVES,

                      "The Jolly Major."

Lucas's eye sparkled with delight upon perusing this agreeable document. Here was an opportunity of distinguishing himself, equal to, if not greater than that of taking a fortress.

"By H——," said he, "the Jolly Major is right—I am a made man sure enough, if I can secure this fellow, who is the terror of the country, and there is not a moment to be lost ; now that he is wounded, he will be able to make no defense, and I shall have him. Pugshy, it is very fortunate that I got home in time. That journey to Dublin was a bad business. You know that I went to attend my uncle's funeral, with a hope that I might come in for a good property, and what do you think. but the old scoundrel had not left me even a shilling to buy a rope, and be d——d to him. Here have I lost four days by it, and it is even very fortunate that I happened to arrive in time to-day to receive this letter."

"Is it possible he left you nothing, sir?"

"Not a penny! he said in his will that he heard a bad account of me, and so he has left all he was worth to my brother. However, it's one comfort that I don't stand in need of it. I am wealthy enough, as it is. Pugshy," he added, "how is that girl getting on?"

"Troth, sir," she replied, "I'm afeared I carried the matter too far: she's in a bad way."

"What! I hope you have not starved her to death, have you."

"No, sir; but in troth she's pretty near it; she must get some nourishment."

"Go then, and get her some food; not much, observe; keep her pretty easy till my return; I·am called out on immediate duty, but I shall not be many hours away. In the meantime, I will secure this skean and bring it with me. Who knows but it may be serviceable if we come to short grips. Major Graves is to call here in the course of the day, so I will leave you my keys, for you know the thirsty old fellow will not sit dry-lipped in my absence."

"Throth, I know that, sir," replied the wretch, "but then, sure, it isn't for nothing that he's called the Jolly Major. As for the girl, she must get something to eat, or she can't live. I did not think myself she was so far gone until to-day."

"Well, then, give her food—just what will keep a little strength in her. Curse you, do you think I wanted to starve her outright? I intended to see her to-day; but now I havn't time for that—in fact, I intended to have seen her the moment this dagger was secured, only just now I have other work be fore me—work that you shall soon hear of, Pugsby; aye, and the world, too."

He immediately put on his uniform, ordered out twelve men, and in a very brief space of time they were on their way to the Four-Mile-House—which was a kind of carman's inn—between Dundalk and Newry.

After he had gone, the old woman, now alarmed at the condition in which she had left their intended victim, returned to her room with a small portion of boiled chicken and some bread; she also brought a little weak wine and water, which she knew would be useful in restoring her strength and spirits. On entering the apartment she was astonished at the wild and frantic look of her eyes—yet the very wildness was woful and gloomy, and the frantic expression was that of a person in whom the powers of life were fast ebbing. Every now and then she put her hand to her bosom, and seemed to search for her skean; and not finding it, she uttered a feeble scream, which in a moment was followed by the miserable laughter we have described. That she might have borne her death from mere starvation with calmness and resignation, there is little doubt; but this resignation was impossible when we reflect upon the outrage which she dreaded, and which mingled its horrors with her physical sufferings.

"Here, dear," said the woman, assuming a kind tone, "you have been made to suffer too much; here is a little food for you; but I can't give you much at a time, bekase they say it might kill you. Here, take a little bread and chicken, and some weak wine and water, and it will refresh and strengthen you."

She looked into the woman's face, but did not seem to understand her. The moment, however, her eyes rested upon the food, the instincts of nature came to her relief, and acted as a substitute for reason. She looked imploringly at the woman, and, stretching out her feeble arms, exclaimed:

"Oh, give me—give me, save me, save me."

The other then assisted her to partake of the food, but in great moderation, after which she gave her a little of the wine and water. When she had partaken of these refreshments, she looked up into the old woman's face, and putting forth her hand, she took that of the other in her's, pressed it, and before she let it go the obdurate old crone felt a few warm tears fall upon it. She started as if touched by, as it were, the shadow of some human emotion; for, with a hideous grimace, she said :

"Well, I wasn't always so hard-hearted, and all that I did suffer long—long ago, and all that drew me to wickedness, was the false tongues of my own kind, the foul tongues—the black tongues of women. They first took away my good name, and then I had nothing to guard, and nothing to do, but to be revenged on them whenever I could, for the rest of my life   I will now leave you, and when I think you can take it wid safety, I will bring you more food   It wouldn't do to overreach the mark either," she said in a low tone—which the other could not hear ; after which she left her to herself.

Early that morning the family of the M'Mahons were seated at a melancholy breakfast, for we need scarcely say, that neither tide nor tidings of the fair Rose of Lisbuy could be heard by any of those who felt an interest in her recovery. At that moment her friends were hopeless, and knew not on what hand to turn in order to continue the search for her. Whilst in this mood, a person having the appearance of a well-dressed country gentleman rode up to the door, alighted from his horse, and entered the house. As the usual mark of respect in such cases, the whole family stood up from their meal, but the gentleman at once insisted that they should resume their seats and finish their breakfast.

"I am come," said he, " in consequence of a rumor which I

have heard concerning the abduction of a respectable female in this neighborhood—a daughter of a man named Brian Cal lan, I think."

"It's too true, sir," replied old M'Mahon, "unfortunately, too true. We have searched everywhere—so has her poor heart-broken father's family—but can't find a mark or token of her any more than if the ground had swallowed her. God help us! this unfortunate day, sir. My son, who was on the point of being married to her, is breaking his heart about her; but what's to be done undher God, we don't know."

"I thought at first," said the son, "that it was that no-torious profligate, Cornet Lucas, who was at the bottom of it, because he had designs on the girl before; but then, we went to the barracks, and the Colonel satisfied us that there was no party of men ont on the night she was taken; ay, and it's clear enough, too, that the Cornet himself was at home on the same night, for he proved it by witnesses; and yet, somehow, I am not satisfied,—I know the villain he is."

"Well," replied the gentleman, "I have only to ask if you can bring a horse and pillion to the head inn of Armagh. Can you do this?"

"Why, certainly," replied old M'Mahon, "I will go myself. We have as good a pillion as there is in the parish, and three stont active horses, if one won't do."

"No," replied the stranger, "your son himself must go, and let him wait in Keenan's inn until he receives orders how to act; and when he receives them let him act npon them quickly. I am myself engaged in this matter for the government of the country, who, although you are not aware of it, have taken the business up. It is supposed that she is with the great Rapparee, and I am upon his trail."

"I don't think, sir," replied the son, "that the Rapparee has anything to do with it—and I'd swear he has not. He never yet, they say, committed an outrage upon any woman, but always made it a point to protect them. Even if he did take her though, it surely is not to the town of Armagh he would fetch her."

" Who said she was in the town of Armagh?" asked the gentleman : " I'm sure I did not. I only desired you to get ready a horse and pillion, and to repair to Keenan's inn, and wait for further orders. If you have such confidence in the Rapparee, why don't you apply to him to restore her ?"

"If he knew the circumstances," replied young M'Mahon, "I am sure he would if he could."

" Ay, *if he could,*" returned the gentleman—" you did well to make that condition ; but I believe he has enough to do to take care of himself. At all events, if you choose to be guided by my advice, do so ; if not, follow your own course."

" I will certainly take your advice," replied the young man, "and will be in Keenan's inn very soon. I don't intend to let grass grow under us, at any rate."

The gentleman then bade them good morning, and young M'Mahon having saddled a stout horse, and placed a pillion behind him, was almost immediately on his way to Armagh.

" Arrah, Pether," said Mrs. M'Mahon to her husband, as he sat in a thinking mood, smoking his after-breakfast pipe "who on earth do you think that strange gentleman can be ?"

" I have been thinking of that, Mary," replied her husband, "but I can make nothing of it."

" Arrah, would it be *him.*"

" *Him !* the Lord help you, woman ! didn't I see him two or three times when I was payin' my tribute to him. Oh, no, Mary ; whoever it may be, it's not *him.* You know it was only the day before yestherday that they say he was hunted for his life by Captain Nisbet and the sogers. Poor fellow he has other things to think of than Rose Callan."

"I declare there's something in it, then, or why would he desire Con to bring a pillion behind him?"

"God knows!" said her husband; "from what Con tould us the other night about the robbers he met, I wouldn't be surprised if he was at the bottom of it."

"But Con says it wasn't him he met."

"Neither it was, bekase Con knows him betther than I do. You know that it is Con who generally pays him his tribute. God knows, as I said, who it can be. We must only hope for the best. Con won't be long, at any rate, till he's in Armagh."

CHAPTER VII.

I͞N the meantime, Armagh, in the course of a few hours, was the theatre of a very different scene. Lucas had been about an hour or so gone. His man-servant and the old woman were enjoying themselves over a pot of strong beer, now, as the proverb has it, "that the house was their own," and everything was very quiet in the barracks.

"Pugshy," said the man, "how is the Cornet's affair getting on? Will the garrison surrender, eh?"

"No," replied Pugshy, "till she's made to surrendher—as made she will be."

"Well now, Pugshy, listen to me! Here's your health, you blasted Witch of Endor! I never was a saint any more than yourself; but curse me if, in my worst days, I ever was such a sinner. Now, listen! If you had one drop of honest woman's blood in your parchment old veins, you wouldn't treat that poor girl as you have done; you wouldn't lend yourself to such damned and cowardly villainy, you infernal ould hag.'

"And listen you!" she replied, her withered features becoming frightful from some venomous poison which seemed to stir itself into hideous life within her,—"*listen you!*" It was the family of that girl that ruined me and mine. In the wars of Cromel they fought against the Parliament; and bekase we—that is, my family—were Presbyterians, and assisted Cromel at the siege of Droghedy, where some o' them, they said, wor murdhered by us, they took revenge upon us afterwards, and burned us out o' house and home. I'm now payin' them back in their own coin, or worse coin. *She* doesn't know that, nor would I tell her anything about it, only I put the thing upon a different footing, although I wasn't far from the

truth even in that. I had very little mercy from my own kind.
but was hunted down, and by no one so much as the grand-
mother of this very girl."

"Yes, but this poor girl is innocent."

"I know that; but then hasn't she *their blood in her
veins?*"

This wretch was certainly a strong evidence of the consequences of civil strife; and we are sorry to say that, even up
to the present period, the feelings engendered by it are still
the source of discord and political animosity between parties.
We know that among hundreds of thousands, from whom the
very memory of the facts and outrages has been blotted out
by time, the dark but bitter principle resulting from them still
remains as a curse to the country.

At this stage of their dialogue a knock, having something,
as it were, jolly and authoritative in it, came to the door of
the room in which they sat; for, be it known to the reader
that, as the drink was at their master's expense, they had
deemed it an act of ordinary prudence to bolt the door. In a
moment everything was put aside, both the drink and glasses,
and Tom very demurely opened the door, when who should
enter but the jolly Major Graves. Tom had never seen him
before; but the moment he appeared, Pugshy recognized him
at once.

"Oh, Tom," said she, "bring back the things, it's only
Major Graves; and, Major dear, how is every tether length
of you; and throth I'm right glad to see you, for it's always
holiday time when you come. Tom, get out the things again;
there's no heedin' nor need of heedin' before the Major."

"You're welcome, sir," said Tom, with something of detection in his grin, notwithstanding. "I've often heard my
master talk of you. Pugshy and I, sir, were takin' a glass
of beer, and talkin' over things as they go."

"Well," replied the Major, "what's your name; Oh, Tom! Well, Tom, my good fellow, let me be no hindrance to either your enjoyment or chat; which of you has the keys? because whilst you are at your beer, I must have a bottle of claret, and no man knows better where to find it than myself. Oh, thank you, Tom; what a devil of a lot of keys you have! But no, I'm somewhat jaded; get the claret yourself. Pugshy, go and find me something to eat."

At this moment a gigantic countryman put his huge face into the room, and said:

"May I come in wid de rent, sir?"

"No, sir; get out, you swab, and shut the door. I'll receive your rent by-and-bye, but not till I've got something to eat and drink first. Stand outside there; I'll call you in when I want you. It's a giant tenant of mine, who came into town to pay me rent, and I may as well receive it, and write him a receipt here?"

"To be sure, Major—to be sure; but, holy man, Major darlin', if the beard on your upper lip and your whiskers, aren't a world's wondher for beauty!"

"Oh, Pugshy, my good old lady, I wouldn't part with those whiskers this moment for the king's commission. So this is the claret?"

"It is, sir; and I suppose you know the value of it."

"I ought, Tom, because it was I who got it for him. What's this, Pugshy? Cold fowl—the very thing I'm fondest of; and ham, too. Tom, cut me a slice or two of that ham. Thank you! I like attention and respect, and always reward it. There is half-a-crown for you, and another for you, Pugshy; and now I'll have my luncheon in comfort. Pugshy, I met your master a little out of town; he told me he was going to secure this terrible Rapparee, that won't allow honest people to sleep quietly in their beds—the robbing rascal. He had

a party of twelve men with him, and there is no doubt at all
but he will come home a made man. Here's that he may
succeed as *I* wish!"

"Troth, sir," said Pugshy, "it's very well he was back from
Dublin in time. He went up four days ago to his uncle's
funeral, hopin' to come in for a haul."

"Well, but did he?"

"No, sir; devil a farden he left him—not, as he says himself, even a shillin' to buy a rope to hang himself wid."

"Upon my soul, then, that was a pity, Pugshy," replied the
Major, dryly. "Is he long home?"

"He wasn't half an hour in the house, sir. He had only
time to write a letter, when the news about the Rapparee
reached him."

He then took three or four glasses of claret, and helped
himself to the ham and chicken; after which he leaned back
in the chair and said, with a comic and significant glance at
the old woman:

"Now, Pugshy, for the secret and the girl. I must see
her."

"Oh, I couldn't do that, Major," she replied. "I promised
solemnly to let nobody see her; for he tould me if I did he
would take my life."

"I know he did, for he told me so; but he desired you,
through me, to allow *me* to see her, and to reason with her;
and it will go hard if I don't drive all this nonsense out of her
head"

"I couldn't do it, sir; I must be faithful to my duty. You
know the Cornet's rich, and will reward me well for following
his ordhers. No, sir; barrin' he gave you a token, I couldn't
think of it."

"That's precisely what he said. Unless I give you a token,
Major, that faithful old creature will never let you lay an eye

on her. The token, then," said he, "is tha. she is in the ninth room from the corner of the range. So now are you satisfied?"

Pugshy paused for a minute, and then, reckoning the rooms in her own mind, upon her fingers, exclaimed :

"Well, it's true enough, sir ; nobody but himself or me could tell you that. It will be useless, at all events, for you to speak to her. She would 'a stabbed the masther with a skean she had if he had come near her; but I took it from her to-day, because she was so weak that she couldn't prevent me. The masther brought it with him when he went out. He desired me, when he was goin' to Dublin, to starve her into compliance : and, indeed, I was near carryin' the joke too far. You'll find her in a poor state, sir."

"The joke, Pugshy,—ah, the joke ; but, indeed, it would have been a very good joke if it had succeeded ; but perhaps it *has* succeeded—eh, Pugshy ?"   •

"Not yet, sir, at any rate ; but it's hard to tell what might— hem ! only the masther was called away to-day so suddenly."

"Well, get your key, Pugshy, and let us see her. Reason and common sense may do a great deal, you know. Come, Tom, you may accompany us till we have a glance at this famous beauty."

On leaving the room they found the colossal countrymar still waiting outside.

"Goliah, my man," said the Major, "I will take your rent, and give you a receipt in a few minutes. I am going down to room number nine, here—a lucky number they say--and will be back presently."

Goliah grinned significantly, and they proceeded together to visit this unfortunate girl.

Before they enter, however, we must attempt to afford the reader some intimation of what her sufferings had been previous to their appearance in her room. It is very well known by those who have been reduced to the very last gasp by a long starvation that toward the close of it all bodily pain ceases. thus very much resembling mortification when it sets in in a vital part. There is nothing then experienced but a general collapse and a gradual decay of all strength and feeling, which passes slowly, and without pain, into the unconscious torpor of death. When a little relief, however, in the shape of food is administered—if this be not frequently, but in small quantities, repeated from time to time,—the powers of the system, awakened, by the nutrition already received, into new life, as it were, become sharpened into a state of the most exquisite torture, by an incessant demand for food. This is the worst and most terrible state and stage of starvation ; and in this state did the Major and his two companions find the object of his search.

As they entered, and indeed before, they heard her melancholy cry for food ; and the moment she saw them the same cry was repeated.

"Oh, food !" she exclaimed ; "food—food, for the sake of God ! and, as you expect happiness, bring me food ; for I cannot bear what I suffer. All I *did* suffer is nothing to this !"

"Will you be obedient then ?" said the crone. "If you do, you will get food."

"If I do," said she, clasping her hands, and looking toward heaven, "may the Almighty strike my name out of the list of mercy ! Oh, great God ! vouchsafe to grant me strength, for I have no friend !"

The Major reasoned with her, using the same logic as the old woman, but still received the same reply ; and still she called for food.

"Tom," said the Major, "go instantly and fetch her food, and a little wine and water."

"I'm danged," said Tom. "if I had known this, I'd have put an end to it, let the consequences be what they might Have patience, poor girl; I will bring you food."

While he was absent the worthy Major walked to and fro the room, giving such glances at the old woman as we need not describe. When he returned the Major himself helped her moderately, and also gave her a portion of the claret diluted with water, after which the insatiable cravings seemed to be appeased, and she felt more at ease. The Major then stepped to the door, and beckoned to the man he called Goliah to come down. "Goliah," said he, as he came in, "we want a cast of your office here." And as he spoke he locked the door and put the key in his pocket. "Tie and gag the man-servant immediately. Don't be alarmed, Tom," he added; "beyond this you shall experience neither hurt nor harm at our hands. Submit quietly, and it will be the better for you; but if you make a noise that giant will strangle the breath out of your body. Neither do you be alarmed, Miss Callan; we are your friends, and have come to release you from this cruel captivity, to which the dastardly villain Lucas brought you by an outrage for which he will pay dearly before he sleeps."

"I will not resist, sir," said Tom, "because I cannot blame you for what you do."

In a few minutes he was tightly tied neck and heels, and gagged in such a manner that he could not utter a syllable if his salvation depended on it; and by the time this was accomplished the infamous old crone found herself in the same state, the worthy Major, with his own hands, having afforded her that consolation.

"Now," said he to Rose, "remain as you are for a little, and we shall return for you. Go down to Keenan's, John," said he, addressing the giant, "and bring up the horse and

pillion ; and if any one should question you, say they belong to
Major Graves. Be quick."

John disappeared ; and the Major, taking up the bunch of
keys which the servant had left upon the table, tried such of
them as he imagined might fit into the *escrutoire* in which
Lucas kept his money. None of them fitted in, however ;
upon which he drew a skeleton, or false key, out of his pocket,
and deliberately opening the desk, took therefrom the sum of
three hundred pounds, principally in gold. Having secured
this, he locked it up again, and left it to all appearance precisely as he had found it. In a few minutes the man he called
John arrived at the door with the horse and pillion, and the
Major returning to Rose, said :

"Now, my poor girl, you come with me ! I am setting you
at liberty—releasing you from the power of one of the most
infamous scoundrels that ever disgraced humanity as a man, or
his Majesty's commission as a soldier."

" But who are you ?" she asked. "You are a stranger to
me, and I am afraid of you. Indeed, I am afraid of every one
—God help me. I hope you are no friend of this villain.

He stooped, and whispered a word into her ear, upon which
her eyes literally danced with delight.

"Praise be to the Lord of Heaven !" she exclaimed, clasping her hands, and looking upward. " Oh, take me away, for
I know that, *as a woman*, I can trust in *you*."

He immediately wrapped her cloak about her, put on her
bonnet with his own hands, and taking her up in his arms, as
one would a child, he brought her outside the door, which he
locked, and having afterward thrown the key under the grate
of the Cornet's room, bearing her still in his arms, descended
the stairs, and mounting the horse, she found herself on the
pillion behind him, having been placed there by his gigantic
attendant.

"Now, John," said he, addressing him, "you go quietly out, and join our friends at the appointed place. As for the completion of this exploit, the greatest difficulty, perhaps danger, is yet before me; but I think I have provided for it."

The gigantic countryman then walked out of the barracks; and the Major was about to follow him, when, having arrived at the gate, he was challenged by the sentinel, who put the muzzle of his gun against the horse, and desired his rider to stop.

"You cannot go out, Major, unless by yourself; and, at all events, not with *that* girl. The orders of my commanding officer are against it."

"Who is he?"

"It was Cornet Lucas, sir, who set the guard, after his return from Dublin."

"I know all that," replied the Major. "I met him on his way out with his party to take the Rapparee; but I tell you, sentinel, that *this* business "—and he nodded over his shoulder at Rose—"is likely to get him into a scrape. The Colonel has been put on the scent of it, and there's likely to be an investigation, which is likely again to end in a court-martial. Do you understand that? As for me, I saw the Cornet to-day, and I'm trying to get him out of it; and for that reason he has allowed me to take my own way in it. Do you understand that again?"

"I understand nothing, sir, but my orders. If I committed a breach of duty for any one, Major Graves, I would for you; because it's not the first time you have enabled me to drink your honor's health."

"No, nor it won't be the last," replied the Major. "You know the Cornet's handwriting, don't you?"

"I do, sir, as well as my own."

"Now, sentinel, I only tried you, and I honor you for the

strict discharge of your duty. Your conduct is highly credita
ble. I'm an old soldier myself, and upon my honor, had you
permitted me to bring this girl out without your master's written warrant to that effect, I would have reported you to him.
There's the warrant. Read it."

The sentinel accordingly read as follows :

" *To the Sentinel on guard at the barrack-gate of Armagh :*

" Permit my friend, Major Graves, who is in my confidence,
and by whose advice I wish to act—in a certain matter—to
leave the barracks in company with any female he wishes to
bring with him, without let or hindrance, or question asked.

" WILLIAM LUCAS,

" Cornet in His Majesty's," etc., etc.

"Do you understand anything *now?*" asked the Major,
laughing.

" Oh !" replied the sentinel, " that alters the matter ; pass
on, Major. And I say, your honor, I was *at* the business that
night, and I thought it a piece of stark madness to bring her
here."

" Mark me, sentinel," replied the Major ; " you say you
were *at* the business. Now, sooner than acknowledge that fact
again, go and cut the tongue out of your own head, and give
all the fellows that were there the same caution. There will
be the devil to pay and to flog about it. There's half-a-crown
to drink my health."

" Thank your honor. Pass on, Major."

The Major rode quietly to Keenan's inn, and as he went
along he addressed his companion as follows :—

" Now, my dear girl, in order that you might place confidence in me, and feel that I was your protector, and no friend
or confederate of that scoundrel Lucas, I had no scruple in

communicating my name to you: but on this subject I have a
request to ask. Will you grant it?"

"If I can do it with honesty and propriety, sir, I will indeed—indeed I will."

"With honesty," replied the Major, smiling; " with *honesty*—ahem! Well, be that as it may, I know you at least
are honest. My request, then, is this—that you will not
breathe the name of the man who saved you from that villain,
and rescued you from his clutches, to any living individual
until you receive permission from myself. Call me Major
Graves. To no human being will you mention it."

"Ah, sir," she replied with emotion, "it would be bad, indeed, and ungrateful on my part if I didn't do that much for
the brave man that has saved me from destruction and shame,
and my family, ay, and others too, from broken hearts. Sir,
I take God to witness, I will never breathe your name as the
man that delivered me from worse than death, until I have
your own consent for it.

"That will do, my dear girl," said he, "I am perfectly satisfied."

On reaching the inn he alit, and was met by young Cor-
M'Mahon, who felt amazed at seeing a man in a military un-
dress instead of the gentleman whom he expected.

I suppose," said the Major, "you are the young man who
was about to be married to this girl. A gentleman—a government commissioner, or something of that sort, who was at
your father's house to-day, got me to come and release the girl,
which I have done. She is ill, but bring her in and let her
have some moderate and nutritious food; but mark me—not
much, unless you intend to injure her. It is creditable in the
government to have interfered in this matter, but it is not
creditable to the British army to maintain a state of discipline
in which such outrages can occur without discovery. In *my*

corps, nothing so shameful and atrocious as this could happen. Take her, now; she is as pure and virtuous as when you last saw her. Farewell both; God bless you, and may you be as happy as I wish you!"

His own horse was then brought out, and having mounted him, he rode at a smart trot out of the town by the Newry road.

As to the jolly Major's further movements, the reader need make no further inquiry about them. He often moved in an eccentric orbit, and, like Sir Boyle Roche's bird, seemed to be in two places at the same time. The scene now changes to the Four-Mile-House, already alluded to, where three or four stalwart-looking men, who appeared to belong to one company, sat with liquor before them, along with some other chance customers, to whom the men we mention seem to be strangers. They looked rather grave and demure, but if closely examined, a keen spectator would have said that there was a daring, if not a reckless and desperate expression in the eye and countenance of each.

"Is it true," asked one of the chance customers, "that the great Tory is dead at last?"

"So report goes," replied another; "they say Captain Nisbet wounded him, and that although he escaped from them at the time, he's dyin' for all that."

"Who do you mane by the great Tory?" asked one of the other men; "do you mane the Rapparee?"

"To be sure I do, who else—poor fellow!"

"Faith and the country will be well rid of him," he replied; "he has kept it in sich a state of terror and alarm for as good as five or six and twenty years, that an honest man, especially if he had money, couldn't sleep safely in his bed for him. As for myself I'm main glad to hear that there's an end to him and his robberies. Where was there a gentleman's house, or a nobleman's castle that hasn't beer garrisoned as if it was in a state of siege, in conseqnence of him and his gang—the thieves."

" It's very well, my good friend," replied the other, " that neither he nor any of his men hears you spakin' the same words. He wasn't so bad as you say."

" What I say is truth," returned the other, " and where's the man can deny it ? Is there a man in the two provinces of Ulsther and Leinsther worth fifty pounds in the world, that's ot forced to keep arms in his house, and to fortify it every way he can before he goes to bed ? And don't the gentry of the counthry sleep with a pile of blunderbushes and other arms on a table beside their beds, and a candle burnin' on it all night ?"

" Well, I believe it 'ud be useless to deny that same, sure enough," said the man, " but every one knows that he was kind and generous to the poor. Faith, neighbor, say what you will, I'm very sorry for him, and my own opinion is, that he'll be a great loss to the country."

" I hope you're none of his men," said the other sharply, and with something like suspicion.

" No," replied his eulogist, " and maybe he has betther men than me, and maybe, too, he'd be a different man to-day from what he is or was, only for the cursed laws of the couutry."

" Ay," said another of the strangers, named Shane, it woul' seem, for so his companions called him, " Ay, indeed, devil re shave de one o' dem tieves but as soon as dey take to de high way, but laves it aul on de poor harmless laws—de craturer Ho—ho, dat's a fine excuse for a robber. It' very like de stor, dat I heard of de wolf and de lamb, poor ting. Dey breaks de laws first, and den dey quarrels wid 'em."

" Well done, Shane, let him answer that if he can," said one of his companions.

"Well, but wasn't he first outlawed," replied the other 'and couldn't appear at large in the country?"

"Outlawed!" said Shane, "faix den it was full time for him to be ontlawed, for he let daylight through one o' de king's fellow-shubjex. However, God be good to his sowl if he's dead, and to his body if he's livin', and I say this bekase I'm a Chrysteen man, and wishes well to my inemies."

At this stage of the conversation the landlord came in—a red-headed Milesian, with a face freckled almost into scales, a pair of deep-set, cunning eyes, and a saddle nose, under which opened a cavernous mouth, that displayed an enormous *chevaux de frise* of strong, ill-sorted tusks, yellow as saffron.

"Neighbors, there's something stirrin' abroad in the country ; here is an officer with a party of sogers, and I think I know who they're lookin' for ; but thanks be to goodness, he's not here. The d—d villian, I wouldn't for his weight in goold that he was found in my house."

"What villain do you mane?" asked the apologist of the Rapparee.

"Why, the Tory that was shot by Captain Nisbet's sogers, the Great Robber of the North."

"Well, I think he's not likely to trouble you," said the other; " isn't the man dead or dyin', they say?"

"And I'm glad to hear it," replied the landlord, "only I hope he won't die here. As to that if, he was dead this minute, I'd take my oath his very ghost would rob on the highways."

"In that case," replied his friend, "it would be bad policy to take his life ; he might do more harm dead than livin'."

"At any rate," said the landlord, "there's a report abroad for the last couple of days that he wishes to die in this house, that is, if he's not dead already. It was here in a quarrel he once killed a man, and they say he thinks that, as a punish

ment and penance on himself, he ought to die nowhere else
I'll take very good care he won't die here though,—I might
desart the house if he did ; for divil resave the man, woman, or
child 'ud come near it afther nightfall, the place is so lonely."

They had scarcely concluded when Lucas and his men entered the house, and the former immediately demanded to see
the landlord. This worthy man at once presented himself, and
asked what refreshment his honor and his party required.

"First put those men out," said Lucas, "and after that I
have something to say to you."

"My dear friends, will you plase to go out for a while," said
the landlord ; "his honor has something to say to me."

"But we're travelers, landlord," said one of the knot we
have alluded to, "and as we're tired and intend to sleep here
all night, it's hardly fair to disturb us."

"I am on the king's business, my friends," said Lucas, "and
if you don't disappear in an instant, you shall feel something to
your disadvantage. Get out, you scoundrels, at once !"

"Oh ! on de king's business, God bless him," said Shane :
"bedad we'll do any ting for de king, or to help de sogers, af
dey wanted us. Come boys, we must obey de offisher and his
sogers."

"It's well you did," said Lucas, "otherwise—begone, I say.
Now, landlord," he proceeded, after they had disappeared,
"where is this man ?"

"What man, your honor ?"

"Why, the Rapparee, that's lyir.g wounded in this house."

"Sir, I thank goodness there's no such man here ; or rather,
I'm devilish sorry that there is not."

"You are lying, sir," replied Lucas ; "I see the lie in that
damnable grin of yours, and I give you my honor that if we find
him here, you shall accompany him to Armagh jail. As his
harborer, you are as liable to be hanged as he is."

"I know that, sir," replied the landlord; "but come, let you and your men follow me, and if he is here you must find him."

The whole house was searched—the out-houses were search ed, every nook and corner was searched—the chimneys were searched—every press, chest, and every bed in the house was searched, but without success. There was no Rapparee nor Tory within the premises, and Lucas's indignation at the disappointment was at the red heat after their return to the tap-room.

"I see you're disappointed, sir," said the landlord, in a confidential voice; "but I have something to say to you, only I don't know whether to say it before the men or not."

"Come into another room," said Lucas; and they accord ingly did so. "Now," he continued, "what is it you have to say?"

"Did you get information he was here, sir?"

"Why do you ask that question?"

"Bekase, if you did, the information wasn't far wrong. He *was* to be here, and he *is* to be here—and if I'm not mistaken, he'll be here this evenin'."

"How is that?"

"Why, sir, his friends have given it, that he's either dead or dyin,' in ordher to prevent any search for him; but I believe the truth is, he's only slightly wounded; for how could he escape from Captain Nisbet's soldiers if they had wounded him severely?"

"That's very true," said Lucas; "but then, why should he wish to come here?"

"Ah, sir, you don't know the cunning of that man. He think's he'll be safer in a house like this, bekase it's the last place that anybody would think of searchin' for him, and that he can stay here till he recovers. I'm glad you came, sir You've saved me trouble; for, I tell you, that if he had come

9

here, I'd have had the knowledge of it in Armagh barracks
as fast as man and horse could carry it."

"In the present case, what would you have me do, then ?"
asked Lucas. "Do you think he will be here in the course
of the day ?"

"Why, as to that, you know, sir, that as I'm in none of
his saicrets, it's impossible for me to say ; but I think, from
what I hear of his cunning, that it's very likely—and for that
raison, I'd recommend you and your party just to stop where
you are until evening."

"Yes ; but don't you think it improbable that he would
expose himself, by coming here in daylight ?"

"Why, sir, it's just bekase no one 'ud suspect him of such
a thing, that he'll come in daylight ; but you know very well
he'll come disguised, if he *does* come. Your plan then is, at
all events, to wait until evenin', so as that you may have the
chances, if they're in your favor."

"Well, under the peculiar circumstances of this affair, I believe, landlord, you are right—and in that case, you had better
prepare something in the shape of dinner for us. We can't
sit here all day with empty stomachs."

"Oh, then, I'm afraid, sir, I have nothing daicent enough
for yez—nothing fit to offer yez."

"Why," asked the other, "what have you got ?"

"Why, then, divil a thing, sir, barrin' ham and fowl."

"And what better could you give us ?" said the other.
"Let it be ready in due time. I only hope the rascal Rapparee will come, and that we shan't have our journey for
nothing."

"Well," replied the landlord "I hope there's no fear o' *that*.
God knows, it 'ud be a pity that you should go home as you
came. Would you accept of a glass of wine, sir, as a treat
from me, wid great submission for tak'n' such a liberty ?"

"No, sir," replied Lucas, somewhat superciliously, "I shall not; but fetch me a bottle, and let the men have something to drink—not much though, for they must keep strictly sober. It's but fair we should do something for the house, at all events. Bring the wine to another apartment; my presence might only interrupt business in your tap-room."

All this was immediately complied with. Dinner in due time made its appearance, Lucas dining in the apartment where he had been sitting, and the soldiers in the tap-room. A considerable portion of the day had now passed, and evening was drawing on. The soldiers, in the meantime, had been plied with more liquor than had been contemplated by their commanding officer. The knot of strange travelers, whom we have mentioned, entered into conversation with them, and as a mark of their respect for the "brave sogers," treated them very liberally, so that when the landlord presented his bill, and received payment from Lucas, the item for liquor did not go beyond what he had ordered them, whilst in the meantime most of them were tipsy.

CHAPTER VIII.

LUCAS was now about to give up all expectation of the Rap
paree, and had thoughts of turning out for barracks, when the
landlord approached him, in a state of great but joyful agitation, saying :

"Well, sir, if ever a gentleman was born to luck, and fame,
and fortune, you are. By the sky above us, he's coming. I
saw, this minute, four men carryin' a sick person down the
road toward the house. Keep quiet, sir, and don't let your
men stir till they come—then pounce upon them."

He had scarcely spoken, when four men bore an old decrepid female into the tap-room, and stretched her upon a
couple of chairs. She was evidently dying, and called aloud
for a clergyman. Lucas, big with expectation, approached
her, but a single glance was sufficient to convince him. Instead of the far-famed Rapparee whom he had expected, there
was nobody ill but some wretched old crone, who was apparently in the last agonies. In order to assure himself, however,
against imposition, he examined her withered arms and hands,
inspected her worn and wrinkled features, and her thin, shriveled neck ; after which he returned to finish his bottle, morti-
fied and disappointed to the last degree. "Some infernal an-
tiquated hell-cat," said he, "the very picture of old Pugsliy
Wallace."

The unfortunate wretch, in the meantime, was calling, in
tones so wild and full of despair, for the assistance of a Protestant clergyman, that she became the subject of general compassion, especially as there was not a minister of that per
suasion within two or three miles of the house. No person,
however, should, under the most desponding circumstances ever

abandon nope. Whilst the poor woman was feebly shrieking for the consolations of religion, a venerable-looking gentleman, far advanced in years, was observed riding past the house, but without any apparent intention of stopping; and that he was of the Protestant church, too, was sufficiently evinced from his shovel hat, and his very canonical costume. This fact was mentioned to the landlord, who at once ran out and acquainted him with the deplorable condition of the dying woman.

"I trust, your reverence, it was heaven sent you on the way," said he; "and at the very nick of time, too—for I see you are a Protestant clergyman, and it is such she is crying for."

The clergyman had pulled up the noble horse on which he rode, and exclaimed :

"I trust it was, my friend : but I am feeble, very feeble, and you must assist me to alight. I am indeed glad of this— poor creature, bring me to her; but stay, I must lean upon you, for, as I said, I am indeed very feeble, my friend, and feel that this poor woman's case will soon be my own."

In this manner they entered the tap-room where she lay; and the parson, having contemplated her for a few moments, raise his eyes with a strong devotional feeling, and, turning round, said :

"My friends, will you be good enough to withdraw for a brief space—it will not be long ; for the parting spirit is just hovering upon her lips ; retire with quietness—no noise ; soldiers, never mind the arms—the noise of removing them will distract and disturb her at this solemn moment, when all should be peace. There now—thanks ; your arms will be safe ; just stand outside, and shut the door. Landlord, do you stay ! Have you any cold water in the room, that I may wet her lips ?"

"Yes, please your reverence," replied that person; "here's a jug full of it."

" Set it over here then, and close the door."

The landlord complied with both his wishes, after which his voice could be heard outside, admonishing and consoling the dying sinner to whom he had been so providentially conducted. At length the ceremony was concluded ; and the company, on re-entering the room, had the satisfaction to see that the mind of the departing woman was composed. She expressed herself quite happy, and very grateful for the spiritual aid she had received.

"Landlord," said the benevolent old gentleman, "it would be kind in you to remove this poor old creature to a bed. There is something profane in seeing a Christian spirit pass to its last account in such a place as this. Remove her to a bed then ; and accept of this to requite you ;" and as he spoke he placed a sum of money in his hands. "You have there," he added, "what will enable you to provide her the necessary comforts which she may require, for the short time she lasts, and for her decent interment afterward. She tells me she was taken suddenly ill on the public road, not far from the house. In this case, it is not improbable that she may still recover If so, landlord, let her have the trifle which I placed in your hands. Pray, where are those soldiers from ?"

" From Armagh, your reverence," replied the landlord.

"Are they accompanied by an officer in command of them ?"

" They are, your reverence."

" I am very feeble ; would you present my compliments, and say I am too weak to wait upon nim, and that I shall take it as a favor if he will come to me here. Say I am the Rev. Doctor Wilson, of Killeeny, and would be glad to see him."

This was done ; and, in the meantime, the sick woman was immediately removed to another room, and placed in a comfortable bed.

"Sir," said the clergyman, addressing Lucas when he entered the room, " I understand you are the officer in command of
this party."

"I am, sir," replied that gentleman.

" Pray, is your *route* for Armagh ? because if it be, I should
feel glad of your escort so far."

" It is, sir," replied the other ; " and we shall feel very happy to afford you our protection."

"Many thanks, sir ; I shall gladly avail myself of it. Do
you soon travel !"

" I think we shall go immediately," replied Lucas. " We
have been waiting here upon a matter of importance for many
hours, and I am beginning to fear that a worthy friend of mine
has suffered himself to be humbugged, and made a regular
cat's-paw of, and myself to boot. Sergeant Wallace, turn out
the men ; and, landlord, my horse !"

In a few minutes he and his twelve dragoons were mounted ;
but the feeble old man was somewhat more tardy ; he leant
upon the landlord to his horse, and was not able to mount him
without his assistance. We may observe that the strange travelers who left the room with the soldiers whilst the clergyman
was engaged with the dying woman, did not again return with
them, nor were they seen afterward about the place. They
had disappeared.

The night was now clear ; and the moon, then in her second
quarter, was only occasionally visible. Still it might be called
a bright night, as the clouds that from time to time obscured
her, were fleecy and transparent. The party nad now ridden
some miles, and reached a lonely part of the road, which was
hemmed in on each side by several ranges of trees. On arriv-
ing here, a band of men came out, right and left, upon them ;
but not until they had sufficient time to have recourse to their
fire-arms ; and it would seem that this delay of the attacking

party was deliberate and voluntary, their object being to dis hearten the soldiers by allowing them to feel that their arms were useless. The landlord, in fact, had, while the clergyman was engaged with the woman, taken the powder out of the pans of their guns, and poured water into the touch-holes, after which he replaced the powder in the pans, lest upon examination it might be missed, and the trick discovered. The soldiers leveled their carbines at them, and fired—but without effect ; nothing resulted but so many flashes in the pan.

" O mother of Moses, we are betrayed !" said Lucas. " Our arms have been tampered with, and are useless."

" Yes, Lucas," replied the decrepid clergyman, seizing him by the collar, with a grip like that of Hercules, " you are betrayed, and shall now suffer for your inhuman and cowardly conduct to the inoffensive and virtuous daughter of Brian Callan." He held a pistol in one hand, as he spoke.

" Seize and disarm every man of them !" he shouted, " I shall take care of their commander. Lucas !" he said, addressing that gentleman ; " if you move a single muscle in the act of resistance, I shall shoot you dead ; otherwise your life will be spared."

The struggle between the Rapparees and the military was but short ; and we need not feel surprised at this, because there were upward of two to one against the latter, most of whom, moreover, were intoxicated, and almost incapable of resistance ; independently of this, the Rapparees were by far the more powerful and desperate men.

" Strip them," said their leader—' every man of them : then tie their wrists tight behind them. Take off coat, waistcoat and shirt; and when that is done, send Goliah here. Now, Lucas," he added, " if you possessed the spirit of a gentleman, or the courage of a soldier, I would myself cross swords with you, and give you a chance. But, in either sense, you have no claim of the kind upon a brave or generous man. None but an inhuman scoundrel, and a coward at heart, would treat any female as Miss Callan has been treated by you."

"I was from home," replied Lucas, "and am not responsible for it. It was contrary to my wishes."

"Was it contrary to your wishes, sir, that she was dragged way in the clouds of night from the protection of her father s roof, with so abominable and brutal a purpose. Now, sir, I tell you that I—*even I*—the Rapparee and outlaw, will have you disgraced as a soldier, and cashiered as a coward and a scoundrel from the British army. The officers of the British army, sir, are—with some exceptions, like you and others— brave men, and gentlemen, and you may take my word for it, they will neither abet nor countenance you as the perpetrator of such an inhuman and revolting outrage as this."

In a few minutes the military was stripped naked from the middle up, each man with his wrists tied so tightly behind him that he could render, neither to himself or others, the least assistance. During the performance of this feat, the Rapparee held Lucas hard and fast, and when it was completed, he said :

"Send Goliah here."

This was the name he had bestowed upon the man known as "strong John M'Pherson," in consequence of his tremend- ous physical powers.

"Now, Goliah," said he, "take this scoundrel and strip him precisely as the others, by far his betters, are stripped. If he attempts to injure you, I will shoot him dead ; and when he is stripped, I will then give you further directions ; but in order to save time, take another man to assist you."

When this also was accomplished, he beckoned to a stout, active-looking little fellow, known among them as "Once Harry."

"Come here," said he, "have you the scourges—the cat with nine tails?"

"I have, sir," replied Harry; "and, upon my sowl, it's I that's ripe and ready to use them."

"Take him over, then," said he, addressing Goliah and his companion; "strap him with a rope against a tree—and you, my little man, give him fifty lashes; neither more nor less."

When Lucas heard this he could keep silence no longer.

"If you be the great Rapparee," said he, "you belie your own character. I have often heard that you were generous."

"Generous!" he replied, proudly—"who dares assert that I am *not?* Yes, sir," he proceeded, "I have performed acts of generosity, of charity, of mercy, that your dastardly spirit could not conceive during a whole eternity. But I am not here to justify my life. I leave that to another tribunal. I am here, however, to punish you, not only for the cruelty you inflicted upon an innocent girl, but for the atrocious and diabolical outrage which you intended. Take him away and punish him."

In less than a minute he was strapped to a tree, as directed, when Quee Harry immediately set to the work of castigation, which he plied with such sincerity and vigor, that the unfortunate sconndrel's screams and howlings might have been heard at an immense distance—tradition states it at that of three miles, as the night, it is said, was calm. When this was concluded, they placed him, bound and bleeding at the head of his men, all of whom were obliged to walk in that degraded state into the barracks of Armagh.

"Here is a skean I got with him," said Goliah. "What the devil could have made *him* carry such a thing?"

"Give it to me," said the Rapparee. "I will return it to the proper owner, who, I trust, will never again be obliged to use it in defense of her honor and good name."

The Rapparee's words to Lucas were prophetic. His brother officers, headed by Colonel Caterson, having been led, by an investigation into the punishment inflicted on him by the Rapparee, to sift the particulars of the outrage which, now that the poor girl was free and in a state of safety, flew like wildfire over the whole country, instituted an inquiry, which ended in his trial by a court-martial, the sentence of which was: "That Cornet Lucas, in consequence of being convicted of conduct unbecoming and disgraceful to an officer and a gentleman, be dismissed the British army." Nor was this all. He was prosecuted for the abduction by her father, aided and supported by the brave and fiery Johnstons of the Fews, and received as punishment a term of two years imprisonment.

Here, now, may the reader perceive, not only the extraordinary talents and fertility of invention, which characterized this remarkable man, but the singular ease and felicity with which he inflicted upon the head of Lucas such a terrible plenitude of vengeance. In the first place, he robbed him of three hundred pounds; next, he robbed him and his soldiers of whatever money they had about them when stripped; then of their clothes, arms, ammunition, and horses, all of which were seized upon as regular and legitimate booty, and as such were they appropriated. But, perhaps, in the catalogue of disgraces which Lucas suffered, the degradation of his being flogged like a felon by the hands of a common highwayman, and driven, we may almost say, into his own barracks at the head of twelve of his own men, tied and stripped naked, was, of all he suffered, the most bitter and penitential to him. He nourished a long and undying vengeance, however, and ultimately lived to turn the tables on the Rapparee;—but no more of this here, as we hope to treat the whole subject on a larger scale.

One evening, about a month after the event we have just described, there was a wedding held at the house of Brian

Callan. The sun shone clear and cloudless, the air was balm, and a mild, serene light lay upon the face of nature. The assemblage was numerous, and every countenance was lit up by a sense of happiness and innocent enjoyment. Callan's house, although large and spacious, was unable to contain the numbers whom the hospitality and kindness of both parties—we mean the friends of the bride and groom—had brought together on the occasion. They consequently adjourned to a beautiful green that stretched beside the house, where they had ample room to enjoy the dancing, which is usual on such occasions. Here healths went round, stories were told, and songs were sung, whilst the merry dance was sustained with agility and vigor. In this state were the individuals who composed this festive and happy meeting, when a well-dressed and very handsome gentleman approached, and after a pause advanced to the bride, whom he bowed to gracefully. Then, turning to her husband, he said:

"Sir, will you permit me one dance with your lovely bride ?"

"With pleasure, sir," replied M'Mahon; "you do her and me an honor."

He then took her out, and danced with a degree of ease and elegance that surprised them all, whilst at the same time, he retained all the steps peculiar to the best dancers among the peasantry. Having concluded it, he led the blushing girl back to her seat, and taking her skean from his breast, he presented it to her, with these words:

"This, you know, is yours; and I feel satisfied that you never will again have occasion to use it in defense of your honor. Keep it as an heir-loom in your family, and as a memorial to your children of their mother's virtue. Perhaps you may also tell them, when I am in the dust, that on your wedding day you had the honor—I will say so—of taking one dance with REDMOND COUNT O'HANLON !"

The Peep O'Day.	The Denounced.
The Croppy.	Peter of the Castle.
The Mayor of Windgap and Canvassing.	Father Connell.
The Bit o' Writin'.	The Ghost-Hunter.
The Boyne Water.	The Life of John Banim.

CATHOLIC CRUSOE. By Rev. Dr. Anderdon 1 25
CATHOLIC LEGENDS 1 00
CATHOLIC SONGS OF THE MONTHS. Verses from Father
Ryan, Father Faber, etc. Full page colored illustrations...net   25
CATHOLIC FLOWERS FROM PROTESTANT GARDENS.
Gilt edges, steel plate. Red line 1 25
CATHOLIC O'MALLEYS..................................... 75
CATHOLIC OFFERING. By Archbishop Walsh............... 75
CARROLL O'DONOGHUE. By Christine Faber. Imitation half
morocco. gilt top..................................... 1 25
CARLETON'S (WILLIAM) WORKS. Ten vols., 12 mo, neatly
bound in leather, half morocco, gilt top, per set............net 7 00
or sold separately, single vols., each ....net   75

Willy Reilly.	Valentine McClutchy.
Jane Sinclair.	The Poor Scholar.
The Emigrants of Ahadarra.	Fardorougha, the Miser.
The Tithe-Proctor·	The Black Baronet.
The Black Prophet.·~	The Evil Eye.

CASTLE OF ROUSSILLON. By Mrs. James Sadlier 75
CARPENTER'S SPELLER. 12mo, boards ...., ...net 10
CHRISTIAN MAIDEN'S LOVE. By Louis Veuillot 75
*CHRISTIAN ARMED, THE. By Father Ignatius (Spencer).
Passionist. Cloth. red edges....... ,.....................   50
CHRISTIAN POLITENESS FOR LADIES AND GENTLEMEN 1 25
CHRISTIAN AND RELIGIOUS PERFECTION. By St. Al-
phonsus Rodriguez of the Society of Jesus. 3 vols., 12mo, cloth,
red edges .... net 2 00
CHRISTIAN MISSIONS. By T. W. M. Marshall. 2 vols., 8vo , net 2 00
CHRISTIAN BROTHERS' THIRD READER. 12mo, cloth, net   32
CHRISTIAN'S RULE OF LIFE. By St. Alphonsus M. Liguori.
Cloth, red edges   50
CHRISTIAN VIRTUES. By St. Alphonsus M. Liguori.......... 1 00
CHRISTIANITY IN CHINA, TARTARY AND THIBET. By
Abbe Huc. 2 vols., 12mo, cloth .. ..net 1 50
CHRISTOPHER COLUMBUS. By Marquis de Belloy. Large
type, toned paper, fine satin cloth, bevelled, gilt edges 2 00
CHRISTMAS NIGHTS' ENTERTAINMENT   60
CHANCELLOR AND HIS DAUGHTER. THE. By Agnes M.
Stewart 1 25
CHATEAUBRIAND'S ATALA. Illustrated by Gustave Doré.
Quarto, toned paper, fine satin cloth, bevelled. Gilt edges..... 2 00
CHIVALROUS DEED, A. By Christine Faber. Imitation half
morocco, gilt top....... ....· 1 25

Catholic Standard Publications.

DUTIES OF YOUNG MEN. By R. A. Vain.................... 75
DUTY OF A CHRISTIAN TOWARDS GOD 50
DUMB BOY OF FRIBOURG. By Anna T. Sadlier 40
DROPS OF HONEY. By Rev. A. M. Grussi, C.PP.S............ 75
DROPS OF HONEY LIBRARY. 9 vols., per set................ 6 75
DYRBINGTON COURT. By Mrs. Parsons..................... 1 25
EASTER IN HEAVEN. By Rev. F. X. Weninger, D. D 1 00
*EASY LESSONS IN IRISH. By Very Rev. Canon Bourke, D. D. 1 00
ELEVATION OF THE SOUL TO GOD. 360 pages............ 75
ELINOR PRESTON. By Mrs. James Sadlier...........:........ . 1 00
ENGLAND.—BISHOP ENGLAND'S WORKS. Two vols. in
    one. Large octavo, cloth. 1,180 pages..................... 8 50
    The same, 2 vols , half morocco...... .... 7 00
EMPIRE AND PAPACY. By M. A. Quinton... .... 1 25
EPISTLES AND GOSPELS. Cloth, red edges.................. 25
ERRATA OF THE PROTESTANT BIBLE (Ward)............. 1 00
ERIN GO BRAGH SONGSTER, paper cover 25
EVENINGS AT SCHOOL. New edition, full page illustrations, net 1 00
EXILE OF TADMORE. By Mrs. J. Sadlier.................... 40
FABIOLA. By His Eminence Cardinal Wiseman. Illustrated :.. 1 00
FABER (CHRISTINE) WORKS. Four vols. Imitation half
    morocco, gilt tops, per set...................... .... 5 00
FAIR FRANCE DURING THE SECOND EMPIRE............ 1 00
FAIRY FOLK STORIES. Full page illustrations, 570 pages.
    Reduced to ....,..... 1 00
FAMILY, THE. By Mrs. James Sadlier...................... 60
FATAL RESEMBLANCE, A. By Christine Faber. Imitation
    half morocco, gilt top.......... .... 1 25
FATE AND FORTUNES OF O'NEILLS AND O'DONNELLS 2 00
FATHER DE LISLE. By Cecilia M. Caddell.................. 75
FATHER SHEEHY, AND DAUGHTER OF TYRCONNELL.
    By Mrs. J. Sadlier. 12mo., cloth, 2 vols. in one................ 1 00
FATHER PAUL AND OTHER TALES........................ 40
FAUGH A BALLAGH SONGSTER, paper cover.............. 25
FEASTS AND FASTS. By Rev. Alban Butler, D. D......... net 75
FEAST OF FLOWERS CLARE'S SACRIFICE, &c............ 75
FIRESIDE STORIES....................................... 40
FIFTY REASONS WHY THE ROMAN CATHOLIC RE-
    LIGION OUGHT TO BE PREFERRED TO ALL OTHERS 25
FLOWERS OF CHRISTIAN WISDOM. Red edges........... 75
FLOWERS OF PIETY Prayer Book). Prices upwards from.... 85

FLORENCE MACARTHY. By Lady Morgan.............. .... 1 50
FOSTER SISTERS. By Agnes M. Stewart. 12mo., cloth........ 1 25
FOLLOWING OF CHRIST. By the Right Rev. Bishop Chal-
   loner. 32mo., cloth, red edges................................ 40
   French morocco or Persian calf, flexible gilt edges............ 1 00
   ᵀollowing of Christ with reflections, 24 mo., cloth, red edges;   50
      Also made in finer bindings. Complete list on application.
FROM ERROR TO TRUTH..... 75
FURNISS' TRACTS FOR SPIRITUAL READING............ 1 00
GEMS OF PRAYER (Prayer Book). Prices upwards from...... 25
GERALD BARRY, OR THE JOINT VENTURE.............. 1 00
GERALD MARSDALE. By Mrs. Stanley Carey.............. 1 25
GERALD GRIFFIN'S WORKS. 10 vols., 12mo., leather, half
   morocco, gilt tops. Per set ....net 7 00
   or sold separately, single volumes...................each, net 75
      Tales of the Munster Festivals.   The Duke of Monmouth.
      Tales of the Five Senses, and   Tales of the Jury Room.
         Night at Sea.
      The Collegians.   The Aylmers of Ballyaylmer.
      The Rivals, and Tracy's   Poetical Works, and Tragedy
         Ambition.   of Gisippus.
      Life of Gerald Griffin.   The Invasion.
GLORIES OF MARY. By St. Alphonsus M. Liguori, over 800 pages 1 25
GOLDEN BOOK OF THE CONFRATERNITIES. Cloth, red
   edges, over 400 pages 50
GOOD READING FOR YOUNG GIRLS....................... 75
GORDON LODGE, OR RETRIBUTION. By Agnes M. White. 1 25
GRACES OF MARY, THE. FOR THE MONTH OF MAY.
   Cloth, red edges, over 500 pages.............................. 60
GREAT DAY, THE. By Mrs. J. Sadlier....................... 40
GROPINGS AFTER TRUTH................................. 60
GRACE O'HALLORAN. By Agnes M. Stewart................. 75
GREEN ISLAND 40
GROUNDS OF THE CATHOLIC DOCTRINE.................. 25
GUARDIAN'S MYSTERY, THE. By Christine Faber. Imita-
   tion half morocco, gilt top 1 25
HANDY ANDY. Large 12mo, illustrated...................... 1 25
HANS THE MISER AND OTHER TALES...................... 75
HAY ON MIRACLES. By Right Rev. George Hay, D. D.,..net 50
HEROINES OF CHARITY..................................... 1 00
HERMIT OF THE ROCK. By Mrs. J. Sadlier 1 25
HEIRESS OF KILORGAN. By Mrs. J. Sadlier................. 1 25
HORNEHURST RECTORY. A Novel............................. 1 50

Catholic Standard Publications.

ILLUSTRIOUS WOMEN OF THE BIBLE AND CHURCH
   HISTORY. By Mgr. Bernard O'Reilly. Full page illustrations 2 50
IRISH FIRESIDE LIBRARY. 6 vols., per set 6 00
  "   NATIONAL SONGSTER. 200 pages 1 00
JAPANESE MARTYRS. By Rev. Joseph Broeckeart, S. J. 75
JESUS IN THE TABERNACLE. Cloth, red edges 50
KEENAN'S DOCTRINAL CATECHISM 50
KEATING'S HISTORY OF IRELAND. By Rev. Geoffrey
   Keating, D. D. 750 pages, gilt edges .... net 5 00
KEEPER OF THE LAZARETTO 40
KEIGHLEY HALL, AND OTHER TALES 40
KEY OF HEAVEN. 18 mo. (Prayerbook). Prices upward from 75
  "   "   "   24 "   "   "   "   "   60
  "   "   "   32 "   "   "   "   "   50
  "   "   "   48 "   "   "   "   "   25
KERNEY'S CATECHISM OF UNITED STATES HISTORY, net 15
KING AND THE CLOISTER. By E. M. Stewart 1 00
KIRWAN UNMASKED. Paper covers 12
LATIN CLASSICS. Expurgated. Part I, net, 40 cts. Part II, net, 50
LADY AMABEL. By Miss Agnes M. Stewart 40
LA FONTAINE'S FABLES. Red Line Edition. Gilt edges 1 25
LAST OF THE CATHOLIC O'MALLEYS 75
LEGENDS AND FAIRY TALES OF IRELAND. Over 400 pages 2 00
LEGENDS OF ST. JOSEPH. By Mrs. James Sadlier 75
LILY'S VOCATION, AND OTHER TALES 40
LITTLE LACE-MAKER, THE; or Eva O'Beirne 75
LITTLE FLOWERS OF PIETY. (Prayerbook) Prices upwards from 25
LITTLE FOLLOWER OF JESUS, THE. By Rev. Grussi, C.PP.S. 75
LITTLE LIVES OF THE GREAT SAINTS. By J. O'Kane Murray 1 00
LOST GENOVEFFA. By Cecilia M. Caddell 75
LOVER'S WORKS. 5 vols., 12 mo. Leather half-morocco, gilt
   tops. Per set, ... net 3 50
   Sold separately, single volumes, each .... net 75
      Handy Andy.   Rory O'More.
      Treasure Trove.   Songs and Ballads.
          Legends and Stories of Ireland.
LOUISA KIRKBRIDE. By Rev. A. J. Thébaud, S. J. 530 pages.. 1 25
LOUAGE'S MORAL PHILOSOPHY. New Edition .... net 75
LOVE. By Lady Herbert 75
LOVE OF JESUS CHRIST. By St. Alphonsus M. Liguori.
   24 mo., red edges 50

Standard Catholic Publications.

Standard Catholic Publications.

MEMOIRS OF DR. R. R. MADDEN. With portrait on steel, net 75
MIRROR OF TRUE WOMANHOOD. By Rev. Monsignor
O'Reilly. 8 vo., cloth, plain edges, 470 pages.................... 2 00
   Gilt edges -- 3 00
MINER'S DAUGHTER, THE. Containing a full explanation of
ceremonies of the Mass, for children. By Cecilia Mary Caddell 75
MISSION CROSS, AND THE CONVENT OF ST. MARY'S.... 35
MISSION AND DUTIES OF YOUNG WOMEN. Rev. White, D. D 60
MISSION OF DEATH, THE. A Tale of the Penal Laws in N. Y. 75
MOORE. Poetical Works of Thomas Moore. 640 pages, royal
octavo. Full gilt sides and edges. Steel portrait............... 3 00
MOTHER'S SACRIFICE, A. By Christine Faber. Imitation
half morocco, gilt top-- 1 25
MOTHER GOOSE MELODIES. Large type edition, Illustrated, 20
MOWBRAYS AND HARRINGTONS. By Mary M. Meline. 75
MONTH OF MARY. By Rev. D. Roberto. Cloth, red edges..... 60
MONTH OF MARY. By Rev.A. Gratry. Introduction by Father Faber 40
MISSION BOOK. 18 mo. Prayerbook. Prices upward from 75
    "   "   24 "   "   "   "   " 50
MYSTERIES OF LIVING ROSARY. Per 100 shee's.............. 2 50
MYSTERIOUS HERMIT. By Mrs. James Sadlier................. 40
NANNETTE'S MARRIAGE. A Catholic Tale.................... 75
NEW INDIAN SKETCHES. By Rev. P. J. de Smet, S. J......... 75
NEW LIGHTS, OR LIFE IN GALWAY. By Mrs. J. Sadlier.. 1 00
NEW TESTAMENT. 8 vo., cloth, embossed...................... 1 50
   12 mo , large type, cloth, red edges 1 25
   18 mo., cloth, red edges.. 50
   24 mo., cloth, flexible...net 15
   Also other bindings and styles. Complete list on application
NEW TESTAMENT (SPANISH) EL NUEVO TESTAMENTO.net 75
NELLIGAN'S SPEECHES AND WRITINGS. Gilt edges...... 75
NEW IRELAND. By A. M. Sullivan. Over 600 pages............ 1 25
NINETY-EIGHT AND FORTY-EIGHT. By John Savage...... 1 00
NOBLEMAN OF '89. By M. A. Quinton. 2 vols. in one. 816 pages 1 50
O'DONNELLS OF GLEN COTTAGE. By D. P. Conyngham LL.D 1 50
ODDITIES OF HUMANITY... 75
*O'GALLAGHER'S SERMONS. 8vo., 450 pages. English & Irish 1 00
OUR COUNTRY. By John Gilmary Shea....................... 50
*OUR LADY OF PERPETUAL HELP. 32 mo. Cloth, red edges 40
OUR LADY OF LOURDES. By Lasserre...................... 2 00
ORAMAIKA. An Indian Story................................ 60

Standard Catholic Publications.

REDMOND COUNT O'HANLON. By Wm. Carleton 75
RELIGION IN SOCIETY. By the Abbé Martinet................ 1 50
RELIGION AND SCIENCE. By Rev. Maurice Ronayne, S. J., net 75
REVELATIONS OF ST. BRIDGET. By Rev. W. H. Neligan, D.D. 60
RECLUSE OF RAMBOUILLET. By Anna T. Sadlier............ 40
RODRIGUEZ CHRISTIAN PERFECTION. 3 vols., red edge, net 2 00
ROME, TheCapital of the ChristianWorld. Rev. W. Nelligan, D.D. 1 00
ROME AND THE ABBEY. A Tale of Conscience................. 1 25
ROME, ITS RULERS AND ITS INSTITUTIONS. J. F. Maguire 2 00
ROSARY BOOK. Paper cover. Illustrated........................ 10
ROBERT MAY AND TOM HOWARD...................... 40
ROSARIO. A Catholic Tale of the Sixteenth Century............. 75
ROSEMARY, OR LIFE AND DEATH. By J. Vincent Huntington 1 50
ROSE LE BLANC. By Lady Georgiana Fullerton............... 1 00
ROSE OF ST. GERMAIN'S, THE. By Agnes M. Stewart....... 1 25
ROSE OF VENICE, THE. 250 pages........................ 75
*RYAN'S POEMS. By Rev. Abram J. Ryan, the Poet Priest of
the South. Large 12mo, fine cloth. 465 pages; 11 Illustrations 2 00

    Quarto Edition, red line, Persian calf, padded, red under
      gold edges...net 4 00
    Also finer bindings. Complete list on application.

RURAL ESSAYS. 8 vo., full sheep, Illustrated, over 600 pages, net 75
RULE OF LIFE. By St. Alphonsus Liguori. Cloth, red edges... 50
STORIES OF OLD NEW YORK, Etc. By Grandfather Greenway 1 25
SAINTLY CHARACTERS. By Rev. W. H. Nelligan, D.D........ 75
SACRED HISTORY. By Bishop Challoner...................... 50
SADLIER, MRS. JAMES, WORKS OF. New and uniform
edition, 14 vols. Per set, in box...........................net 7 50

    Comprising the following volumes:

Aunt Honor's Keepsake.	Elinor Preston.
Blakes and Flanagans.	Hermit of the Rock.
Bessy Conway.	Heiress of Kilorgan.
Confederate Chieftains.	MacCarthy More.
Con O'Regan.	New Lights.
Confessions of an Apostate.	Old and New.
Father Sheehy, and Daughter of	Old House by the Boyne.
Tyrconnell.	

SAVAGE'S POEMS. By John Savage. 12mo., gilt top, 325 pages 2 00

SCOTTISH CHIEFS, THE. By Miss Jane Porter................ 1 00
STRAYED FROM THE FOLD. By Minnie M. Lee.............. 1 25
SCHMID. Canon Schmid's Tales. 135 Illustrations. 6 vols. Per set 8 00
SCAPULAR BOOK. Complete, paper............................ 10
*SCHOOL OF JESUS CRUCIFIED. By Fr. Ignatius; Passionist. 75
SCIENCE AND RELIGION. By Cardinal Vaughan... ....net 75
*SERAPHIC MANUAL. New Complete Edition. Cloth.   net 40
SERAPHIC STAFF. Cloth, red edges............................. 25
SERAPHIC OCTAVE, THE. Cloth, red edges ....net 50
SEMME'S SERVICE AFLOAT. Cruise of the Alabama and
    Sumter during Civil War. 833 pages, oct. Full page engravings 8 00
    Half Turkey morocco.. 6 00
SEVEN OF US. By Marion J. Brunowe................................ 75
SERMONS AND LECTURES OF FATHER BURKE. 3 vols.
    cloth. Over 1,800 pages.................................... 6 00
        Sold separately as follows:
      Vol. I. Lectures and Sermons. Cloth........................ 2 00
      Vol. II. Lectures and Sermons. Cloth....................... 2 00
      Vol. III. Lectures in Ireland. Cloth........................ 2 50
      Cloth, full gilt sides and edges, per volume................. 8 00
SERMONS AND DISCOURSES. By Most Rev. J. MacHale D.D, net 1 00
SERMONS OF THE PAULISTS. Vol. VI. 12mo., cloth........ 1 00
SERMONS FOR EVERY SUNDAY IN THE YEAR. By Rev.
    W. Gahan, O. S. A. New edition, 650 pages. Red edges.....net 1 50
*SERMONS BY ARCHB'P O'GALLAGHER. (Irish and English) 1 50
SERMONS ON OUR LORD AND B. V. M. Cardinal Wiseman, net 1 00
SERMONS ON MORAL SUBJECTS. Cardinal Wiseman, net 1 00
SOPHIE'S TROUBLES. By Mme. La Comtesse de Segur........ 75
SOUTHERN CATHOLIC STORY. By Minnie Mary Lee......... 1 25
SOLITARY ISLAND. 12mo , 400 pages. By Rev. John Talbot Smith 1 00
SHIEL'S SKETCHES OF THE IRISH BAR.................... 1 00
SIXTEEN NAMES OF ANCIENT IRELAND. By Rev. O'Leary 50
SPEECHES FROM THE DOCK. 408 pages, 12 mo., cloth 1 25
ST .JOHN'S MANUAL PRAYERBOOK. Prices upward from... 1 50

SONG BOOKS.

Erin Go Bragh Songster. 180 pages, paper cover................. 25
Faugh-A-Ballagh Songster. 180 pages, paper cover............. 25
Forget Me Not Songster, 300 pages, paper cover.................. 25
Gem Songster, The. 80 pages. Cloth, flexible.................... 10
Harp of Erin, Songster, 300 pages, paper cover.................. 25
Irish National Songster. 360 pages, cloth...................... 1 00
*New Spirit of the "Nation." By Martin MacDermott. 16mo., 50
Universal Irish Song Book. 12mo., 50 engravings. Over 500 pages 1 50
Songs of Ireland and Other Lands. 900 pages, 12mo., cloth.... 1 50
Spirit of the Nation. Young Irelanders, 1848. 84 pages, 16mo., cloth 50

SUNDAY SCHOOL TEACHER'S CLASS BOOK. Per doz., net 96
SYBIL. A DRAMA...net 75
STORIES FOR BOYS... 40
STORIES FOR GIRLS.. 40
STORIES FOR CATHOLIC CHILDREN. By Rev. A. M. Grussi 75
SPEECHES OF CELEBRATED IRISHMEN, IRISH CHAR-
ACTER, Etc. By Henry Giles. 12 mo., 400 pages............. 1 25
STORY OF ITALY. By Rev. A. Bresciani, S. J.................... 1 25
STORIES ON THE BEATITUDES. By Agnes M. Stewart..... 75
STORY OF IRELAND. By A. M. Sullivan. 12mo., 650 pages.
Illustrated,... 1 50

STRAW-CUTTER'S DAUGHTER. By Lady Fullerton.......... 1 00
STATIONS OF THE WAY OF THE CROSS. Paper........... 10
SURE WAY TO FIND OUT THE TRUE RELIGION.......... 25
SPIRIT OF ST. LIGUORI AND VISITS. 275 pages 75
SPANISH CAVALIERS. By Mrs. James Sadlier...... 75
TALES AND STORIES. By Mrs. James Sadlier.................... 40
TALES AND LEGENDS FROM HISTORY...................... 1 00
TEN STORIES. By Mrs. James Sadlier............................ 40
THE LOST DAUGHTER. A Gypsy Tale of the 15th Century... 75
TWO BROTHERS, THE. By Anna T. Sadlier................. 40
TWO BRIDES, THE. A Catholic Story. Mgr. O'Reilly, 12mo.,
415 pages.. 1 25
TWO COTTAGES. By Lady Georgiana Fullerton............... 20
TWO GRAY TOURISTS. By Richard Malcom Johnston........ 1 25
TWO VICTORIES, THE. A Catholic Tale. By Rev. T. J. Potter 1 00
THREE KINGS OF COLOGNE. By Rev. Titus Joslin. 24mo., cloth 30
THOUGHT FOR EACH DAY IN THE YEAR. By a Jesuit Priest 1 00
TRUE TO THE END, AND OTHER TALES.................... 40

Standard Catholic Publications.

www.ingramcontent.com/pod-product-compliance
Lightning Source LLC
Chambersburg PA
CBHW021112020726
47500CB00003B/716